"How would you feel about spending the night?"

Seth couldn't have heard that right. "Pardon me?"

Harper patted the bed next to her. "Sleep with me. Please..."

If he hadn't had a hard-on before, he would have gotten one just from hearing those words. As it was, his body was on red alert. But she'd said *sleep*, and that's probably all she meant. So he shouldn't get too excited.

Wait. Too late.

"Uh, Seth."

"Yeah." Damn. His voice had broken. He cleared his throat and tried again. "Yeah."

She did a little throat clearing of her own. "I'm making you nervous."

"No. Well, yes. But it's okay."

"Get into bed. That'll make things easier."

He nodded. Moving to the other side of the bed, he slipped under the covers. It did make things easier. At least she couldn't see the full extent of his arousal....

Blaze™

Dear Reader,

At the end of *Relentless*, the first book of the IN TOO DEEP... trilogy, one of our guys, Seth, is in trouble. *Big trouble.* And Harper, the no-nonsense doctor who never wanted any part of this fight, has to make a life-changing decision. *Release* is their story, and man, is it emotional.

Personally, I love a great action book where there's danger around every corner and you're on the edge of your seat, but I also wonder, after the thrill ride is over, how the characters deal with the consequences.

This is a book about consequences. About finding out what really matters. About love and what it means. Seth has to learn that he's more than a soldier and Harper, well, she has to learn that she can't hide her heart forever.

In March look for *Reckoning*, the last book in this trilogy, where Nate and Tam face their own day of reckoning.

I'd love to hear from you! You can write to me at aka.jo.leigh@gmail.com or check out my Web site and blog at www.joleigh.com.

Love,

Jo Leigh

JO LEIGH
Release

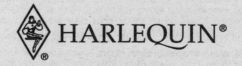

TORONTO • NEW YORK • LONDON
AMSTERDAM • PARIS • SYDNEY • HAMBURG
STOCKHOLM • ATHENS • TOKYO • MILAN • MADRID
PRAGUE • WARSAW • BUDAPEST • AUCKLAND

ISBN-13: 978-0-373-79305-1
ISBN-10:   0-373-79305-7

RELEASE

Copyright © 2007 by Jolie Kramer.

This edition published by arrangement with Harlequin Books S.A.

® and TM are trademarks of the publisher. Trademarks indicated with ® are registered in the United States Patent and Trademark Office, the Canadian Trade Marks Office and in other countries.

www.eHarlequin.com

Printed in U.S.A.

ABOUT THE AUTHOR

Jo Leigh has written over thirty novels for Harlequin Books since 1994. She's a double RITA® Award finalist, and was part of the Harlequin Blaze launch. She also teaches writing in workshops across the country.

Jo lives in Utah with her wonderful husband and their new puppy, Jessie. You can chat with her at her Web site, www.joleigh.com, and don't forget to check out her daily blog!

Books by Jo Leigh
HARLEQUIN BLAZE

*In Too Deep…

Don't miss any of our special offers. Write to us at the following address for information on our newest releases.

Harlequin Reader Service
U.S.: 3010 Walden Ave., P.O. Box 1325, Buffalo, NY 14269
Canadian: P.O. Box 609, Fort Erie, Ont. L2A 5X3

To Barbara Joel and Barbara Ankrum
for being there just when I needed them.

1

SETH TURNER REACHED FOR HIS blanket with a hand that wasn't there. He'd been half-asleep, but now he was awake and filled with a red heat that burned behind his eyes, in his gut. Every day he had to relearn the raw truth: his left hand was gone, ripped apart by a bullet, tossed aside by the doctor upstairs. Without his consent.

He hated her for it. Hated her touching him even to give him an exam. Hated her voice when she tried to convince him she'd done the right thing—saved his life. Did it ever occur to her that he didn't want this life?

He pulled the blanket up with his right hand and settled back on the pillow. It was a different kind of torture, knowing she was sleeping upstairs. That he would have to live here, with her, for months yet to come while he learned to use the prosthesis.

It had already been three months since she'd performed the surgery. It had taken this long for the wound to heal, for his skin to form a useless lump three inches up from what used to be his wrist. He'd been in bar fights, he'd been in wars, he'd even survived Delta Force training, but nothing had been harder.

He understood now why men, good men, turned to drugs and alcohol after they'd been mutilated. The pain was the least of it. The part he couldn't stand, that made him want to die, was the loss of everything that was important about him. Which was the part Dr. Harper Douglas didn't get.

To make things worse, to add the goddamned cherry on top, there were his dreams. They came every night now. At first he'd shaken them off, but there was no use pretending they were going to stop. He woke in the middle of the night sweating and hard, his erection throbbing as images of her, of goddamn Harper, made him ache until, with his one good hand, he took care of business. Even that didn't end his torment. Once he'd come, thoughts of her haunted him long into the pale mornings. With luck he'd fall asleep again, but mostly his luck had run out. By the time she came downstairs he hated her again. He tried to be civil, but it didn't come easy.

Harper, with her no-nonsense attitude and her sharp blue eyes, looked at him as if he were a piece of meat, a patient, not a man. Her in her white robe, tight at the waist and crossing at her breasts. She wore no bra when she came from her bedroom, and though her breasts weren't large, they moved when she did, swaying just enough to sear a picture in his head.

His hand moved down to his erection, and he thought again that he should feel grateful that he'd lost his left hand. He wrote with his right, threw with his right, beat off with it. But his left, that was his rudder, his stabilizer. Without it, how would he use the sniper rifle? Reload? How could he defend himself, let alone kill a man? Shit, he couldn't even tie his shoes.

He heated again as he remembered finding the slip-on loafers that had appeared by his bed. Harper had put his boots in a cupboard and replaced them with grand-dad shoes, something a crip like him could handle.

Shifting again in the hospital bed, he wished for the hundredth time that the bullet had hit him right between the eyes. Not that he'd want to abandon Nate and the others, but Jesus. What was he supposed to do now?

He hadn't even realized that he'd only ever seen himself as a warrior. Not even that—as a weapon. He'd been good for exactly that and nothing else. And now he was broken, a piece of junk to be thrown in the scrap pile.

He closed his eyes and prayed for sleep. What he got instead was a wave of need and the cursed images of Harper torturing his soul.

THE WALLS OF THE house were mostly gone, but the bathroom was still private. Four walls, a ceiling and a door complete with lock. Harper stared at the sink, at the faucet that dripped brown rust instead of water, and all she could think was that she couldn't treat the child with her hands so filthy. The chance of infection was too great. But the water…the water had stopped. The electricity was off. Everything in the tiny village in the north of Serbia was in shambles.

There was no hospital, no other doctors, and she only had the small bag, barely more than a first-aid kit.

The child...he was four, maybe five. He spoke no English, and her Serbian was terrible, so she couldn't ask him where his mother or father was. Maybe they were out there, with the others in the square. But no. She couldn't think about that right now. She couldn't save them, but the child, the boy... Perhaps...

She looked up from the useless sink to see her own image in the cracked mirror. What was she doing here? She could have taken that job at the USC medical center. She could have gone to Africa or Asia, worked with one of the relief agencies or the Red Cross. But she'd gone to the UN. She'd volunteered to go to Kosovo because the war was over, at least officially. She'd never bargained for this. She closed her eyes and breathed as deeply as she could, trying to think of anything but the carnage in the square. There had been so many.

She'd come with Jelka, who'd lived in this village her whole life. Anya, who'd been an excellent aide and a friend. Jelka had come when her mother hadn't answered her phone. Neither had her aunt, her cousins. They'd driven into the square, and the bodies had been everywhere. Harper had known within minutes what had killed them. A nerve agent. Something bad, worse than anything she'd heard of in medical school or the special training she'd received from the peacekeeping force. The men, women and children had died horribly.

She looked at the boy. It didn't matter that her hands were dirty. He was dead. Everything once alive in this town was dead. What she didn't understand was why. No government would sanction this kind of genocide.

No independent army she knew of had the technical ca-
pabilities. Who had murdered Jelka's family? Who had
brought this nightmare into the world?

Harper woke with a gasp, and for a moment she was
back there, in her tiny apartment with its uncomfortable
bed, cracked basin and inconsistent heat. But a few deep
breaths and a sharp focus on the familiar comforter
brought her home to her own bed in her little corner of
East Los Angeles. The shaking would take a little longer.

The nightmares had started months ago and were as
much a part of her life as being a doctor at the free
clinic. She hated them, hated that she woke up sweating
and trembling. There'd been a time, as hard as it was to
believe, when she'd gotten sweaty from a hot man in her
bed. Now the only man in her life was a wounded
soldier living in her basement, cursing her with every
other breath. That is, when he wasn't trying to hide his
hard-on for her.

Nate, Seth—they all told her the nightmares would
end, that she'd have her life back once again, but she
didn't believe it. It was all FUBAR—fucked up beyond
all reason. Every part of it. Especially the man living in
her basement. Seth was a decent guy and she liked him
well enough, she just had no desire to be his den mother.

Okay, so he'd gotten a bum break, but he was alive,
wasn't he? She knew he resented her doing the amputation, but that wasn't unusual. No matter the circumstances, traumas as severe as amputation required long
periods of adjustment. He'd grow accustomed to his
limitations and his prosthesis. The sooner, the better,
because as he was now he was pretty damn useless.

She'd already decided that gainful employment for Seth was just the ticket. They could always use the money, but more than that, he needed to see that he was still productive. Maybe he couldn't be soldier of the year, but there was no way he was going back to that life anyway.

Even if by some miracle they could prove their innocence, how would Seth or Nate or any of them believe in the Army ever again? She knew her country wasn't evil, that it was a small faction of men who believed they were above the law that had caused all the havoc, but her whole world view had been altered irrevocably. That Senator Jackson Raines could publicly call these men, these heroes, traitors to their country…

She shut off that line of thought as she climbed out of bed. There was no use thinking about the mess of a situation. They—Nate, Seth, Boone and Cade, all Delta Force soldiers, along with herself and Kate, the UN accountant who had discovered the dark secret that a Black Ops group from the U.S. had developed a chemical weapon so deadly there was no antidote. They'd escaped with their lives but little else. Bottom line—she couldn't do anything about it, and it was useless to try.

She was a doctor, not a soldier. If she could have completely disassociated herself from the whole matter, she would have. All she wanted was to do her job. To keep the clinic going and lose herself in work. She didn't want to babysit Seth, she didn't want to have to hide, she didn't want to live in this house or have a trauma room in her basement.

Nothing had been right since that one day. Since she'd stood witness to the slaughter of an entire town. Of course she dreamed of it night after night. That day, she'd walked into hell.

Her bathroom floor was cold on her bare feet, but one of the great things about this old house was the water pressure. She turned on the shower, hung her robe and nightshirt on the hook on the back of the door and eased herself under the spray. She thought of nothing but the heat and comfort for several long minutes, then got down to the business of washing.

The more she thought about bringing Seth to work in the clinic, the more she liked the idea. It would get him out of the house, give him a practical way to get used to his prosthetic. And it would be a safe place. The kind of people who came to the clinic weren't likely to connect Seth, especially the way he looked now, to the Wanted posters. She'd encouraged him to do more than grow his hair, but he couldn't stand the mustache or beard. Maybe they could dye his hair, although it would be a shame to change those coppery highlights. Harper smiled, thinking of Seth's reaction if she should dare say such a thing. He wasn't exactly open to his feminine side, was he?

She finished washing her hair, then spread some shave gel on her right leg. She was pasty white, which she'd never been, even as a kid, but she didn't spend much time outdoors anymore. The hiking she loved was a thing of the past, work keeping her a virtual prisoner. It was probably foolish to ignore other aspects of her life, and if it wasn't quite so chilly out, she'd drive herself up to Angeles National Forest and get lost in the trees. Unfortunately this January was exceptionally cold and wet, and she wanted to hike for pleasure, not punishment.

After finishing her left leg, she rinsed off all the soap, shampoo and gel, wishing she didn't have to go down to the basement at all. Wishing she didn't know that Seth was still so angry. Wishing…

Wishing she had a man in her home who wanted her. Wanted to be there. She was lonely. Not because she had no real friends. That was nothing new. She didn't trust a lot of people, not in that intimate way she saw all around her. That had never been her style. But she wasn't one to deny herself when it came to men. She liked them, had always liked them. Not for keeps, of course, but for a month or two. If the chemistry was there, why not?

The chemistry hadn't even been alive in her since that day in Serbia. She didn't even want to think about how long she'd been without. She'd considered Seth, naturally, but he was so…so pissed. At her. Some women might get off on that whole macho anger thing, but not her. Not yet. But if something didn't change, she wasn't guaranteeing a thing.

She grabbed the towel off the rack, and fifteen minutes later she was in jeans and a sweater, her sneakers tied, her hair as neat as it ever got. No makeup, not for work.

Downstairs, the coffeepot had done its job, and she filled two mugs. Black for Seth and light for her. Then she headed down to the basement of doom.

Seth was up and dressed, which he always was, and he was on the floor doing one-armed push-ups. Admirable in any other patient, but Seth took it too far. He wouldn't stop until he reached one hundred. And then he'd collapse, sometimes on his stump, and he would be shaky and weak for too long. All her talk of moderation went in one ear and out the other. Stubborn ass.

She put his coffee down and waited, watching the muscles in his back, the way his butt clenched. From this angle, he was perfect. You had to know him to see that he was one push-up away from a nervous breakdown.

He did the whole collapse thing and, of course, got up too soon. She ignored his red face and rapid breathing completely as she peeled the sock off his stump.

Seth stared over her shoulder, as always. He never complained about how she touched him, but he didn't participate either. It was as if she were working on someone else's body, and that had to stop. Now.

"So how would you like a job?"

He turned sharply. "What?"

"A job. Work. The end of you moping all day."

"What kind of a job?"

"Don't get excited. You don't get to kill anyone. We could use another aide at the clinic."

"Aide?"

She used her hands to feel his stump. The blood flow was good, the scar was healing beautifully. But there was no callous from his prosthetic, which meant he wasn't wearing it enough. "Yeah, stocking the exam rooms, cleaning up, filing. That kind of thing."

He didn't say anything, but the vein in his jaw spoke volumes.

"It's not glamorous, but it'll be good for you. You'll get better at using the hand. It won't replace physical therapy, but it'll accelerate your progress."

"So I can do what?"

"I don't know. Get a life maybe?"

He snorted, which was something she'd grown disturbingly used to. She held his arm to the side so she could examine a bruise that was starting to yellow. "Is this still bothering you?"

"Yeah, a little."

"I'll call Noah."

"For that?"

"Making sure the prosthetic fits perfectly is his job. You won't wear it if it's uncomfortable."

"It's always uncomfortable."

"You'll get used to it if you wear it enough. It's not easy, but you've faced harder things, I'm sure. Don't you want to be able to pick things up? To hold a cup of coffee? Your dick?"

The look he gave her was priceless. She'd only said it to shock him. For a grown man, a man who'd been to war, he sure shocked easily. She probably shouldn't take so much pleasure in making him blush. But he looked good that way, and…oh, God, she needed to get out more. "Let me see you put it on," she said, dropping his arm and replacing it with her coffee, which she picked up easily with her left hand, just to be obnoxious.

He noticed, but he didn't say anything. He just went

about putting on the sock, which he did with his right hand and his teeth, then he got the prosthetic out of the top drawer of the small dresser in the corner of the room.

She wondered if it was uncomfortable for him to sleep here every night. It wasn't so much a cozy basement as a trauma room, complete with portable X-ray, surgical tools, every kind of medicine she could think might be needed and a handy defibrillator. She'd tried to plan for every kind of emergency—and good thing she had or Seth could have died from that gunshot wound.

When Natc had proposed the idea of setting her up like this, she'd been shocked, knowing it would be outrageously expensive. But he'd come up with the money and she'd stocked the basement to the gills. She hadn't had to use it until three months ago. Now it had become Seth's home. She'd offered him the spare bedroom, but he'd turned her down. All he did upstairs was shower and make himself ham-and-cheese sandwiches. She'd never met a more stubborn man. She just wished he'd use that trait to get acclimated to his new life.

He grunted as he struggled with the hand. It wasn't a difficult task, but it was terribly awkward. His left shoulder kept moving, an unconscious response he wouldn't lose for a long time, if ever. There were a million and one things the nondominant hand is used for, and the brain didn't take to this kind of change easily. Finally he was set up, and while the manufacturers tried damn hard to make the fake hands look real, they didn't. They were substitutes, ungainly ones, but in time Seth would find his way.

He looked at her with a surprising lack of satisfaction. "Okay, it's on."

"Open and close," she said, leaning against the long cabinet.

He went through his paces inelegantly, which was to be expected.

"How many hours did you wear it yesterday?"

Seth shrugged. "About five."

"I want you to wear it for a minimum of eight. Which works out well, since that's the minimum you'll be at work."

"I'm not going to be an aide, Harper, so forget it."

"No? What, are you planning to sell your body to earn your keep?"

"If I'm that much of a bother, I'll leave."

"And go where?"

"I can hook up with Nate."

"No, you can't. You'll just be in his way. He doesn't have time to babysit you."

He flushed again, this time with pure anger, but she didn't care. The man needed a reality check. He had to get on with it, just as they all had to get on with it, whether he liked it or not.

"Fine. When do we leave?"

She checked her watch. "Be ready in forty minutes. I'm making breakfast. If you come up in ten, there'll be food for you."

"I'm not hungry."

"Tough. You're going to need your strength. Deal with it."

As she headed for the stairs, she heard him curse her under his breath. She didn't say anything, though. Maybe she was a cold bitch. Hard times called for hard measures.

2

THE FREE CLINIC WAS in a run-down part of Boyle Heights, a sad suburb of Los Angeles where the median income was right at the poverty level, and the people who showed up on the doorstep were a damn sad bunch. They were mostly meth addicts, but there were still the unwanted pregnancies, the search for birth control pills, the folks with the flu and the cough and the red itch "down there." No one came to the clinic if they had somewhere else, anyone else.

All Seth could think about when he walked in the doors was that he'd seen it before. Maybe not this color and maybe there were different posters on the walls, but the poor people all over the world always ended up in rooms like these. With overworked doctors and nurses with sore feet.

If he had to get a job in the outside world, then he supposed this was the safest place to do it. What were the odds that someone here would recognize him? He looked nothing like the man they'd flashed on television or the Wanted picture in the post office. His hair was the longest it had ever been, and the posters didn't mention the missing hand, but that wasn't even it. Since Kosovo, he'd changed. He had lines in his face, around his eyes. He looked tired all the time, and his skin was sallow and pasty. He felt like an old man despite his daily workout.

Now that he was dressed in hospital scrubs, with an old Dodgers baseball cap on his head, no one would pick him out as a soldier or a traitor. He looked at himself in the clinic's bathroom mirror and pulled his cap down a little farther.

He finally understood what Kate had meant when she'd said she'd been invisible as the room-service lackey at the downtown L.A. hotel.

She'd been a forensic accountant for the UN in Kosovo and she'd been the one who'd gotten the Delta Force team involved. She and Nate had been an item, and when Kate had discovered that something fishy was going on, she'd talked it over with him. She hadn't known it at the time, but she'd found the first proof that a faction of the CIA, calling themselves Omicron, had created a mighty nasty chemical agent and they were planning to sell it to the highest bidders, who would then use it to kill whomever they chose—mostly civilians. To add to Omicron's crimes, they'd recruited a Delta Force team, his team—one of the best in the world—to do the dirty work of wiping the evidence off the earth. Their original mission was to go to a secret laboratory in Serbia, collect all the files, kill the scientists working there and destroy the lab. What they hadn't mentioned was that the scientists in that particular lab weren't working on the nerve gas—they were developing the antidote.

Some of the team had escaped—Nate, Boone, Cade and himself. They'd convinced Kate and Harper to come along because they clearly knew too much. The one scientist to make it out alive had been Tamara. She'd come back to the States, and Nate had found her a safe place to do her research. She'd had to distill all the notes from her colleagues to try and recover their progress and then she had to make sure the antidote not only worked but could be dispersed to save whole villages.

Last Seth had heard, Nate was trying to get some money together for more of her tests. He did security work, real high-tech stuff, state-of-the-art, for which he charged a pretty penny. No one complained, as his customers were as shady as they come. A lot of bookies, some conspiracy nuts, an arms dealer or two. But ever since his picture had shown up on Wanted posters across the country, Nate couldn't afford to be picky.

The work had been easier when there'd been two of them. When Seth had been there to cover Nate's back.

Pounding on the bathroom door made him reach for a weapon he wasn't carrying. He closed his eyes and tried to chill, but it wasn't easy.

"You gonna stay in there all day?" It was Harper, of course. "Other people need to use that john."

He gave himself another look in the mirror, then his gaze moved down to the plastic masquerading as his hand. He had to focus to open and close the thing. None of it felt natural or intuitive. But he couldn't hide forever.

He opened the door in time to catch Harper walk into

the cubbyhole she called her office. After he grabbed his regular clothes, he followed her, the scent of cleaning fluid and rubbing alcohol as bright and intrusive as the overhead fluorescent lights.

Her head was bent over an open file as she sat on the edge of a very messy desk. One foot was up on the seat of a plastic chair, and in addition to the stethoscope around her neck, she had a pencil stuck behind her right ear. The pencil looked as if it'd been used as a teething ring.

He wondered again what it was that made him want her. She took every opportunity to bust his balls, and now this. He'd done his fair share of KP, but dammit, a janitor?

She looked up at him for a moment, giving him a quick smile, which surprised him, then she went back to flipping pages with her long, slim fingers. But the smile lingered in his mind's eye. She didn't do it often, at least not when she was with him. But when she did, it made an impact. Maybe it was that one crooked tooth. Everything else about her seemed so perfect, her startling blue eyes, her pale skin and, dammit, even that stupid hair of hers that was not quite blond, too short and always a mess. It all came together to make him want to—

"Seth?"

She was looking at him again. Shit. "Yeah."

"I talked to Noah. He's going to be here in about twenty minutes, so why don't you just lay low until he comes. When he's done, you won't have to worry about being recognized."

"Why not?"

"He's not your ordinary prosthetist. He used to be with the CIA, disguising agents in the field."

Seth felt all his muscles tighten. "You do realize that Omicron is CIA."

"I do. But you don't have to worry about Noah. There's a reason he's not with them anymore."

"So you want me to wear a disguise to work here?"

She nodded. "It's going to be subtle, so don't sweat it."

"Don't sweat it," he said, not understanding her cavalier attitude. "It's not a costume party, Harper. It's my life on the line."

She looked at him with her best doctor-in-charge expression. "I get that. It's my life, too. So stop worrying about it. I'm trying to keep you safe."

He believed she was, but he also believed that she had no idea who she was up against. Omicron would kill every person in her precious clinic if that's what it took.

"Besides," she said, "no one expects you to have only one hand."

He swore under his breath, knowing she was trying to bait him.

She closed her file and stood. As she passed him she touched his shoulder, making him flinch. He didn't think she saw.

"You can do something good here, Seth. You can be useful and get friendly with your new body. Don't screw it up."

He started to tell her exactly what she could screw, but what good would it do? Harper was Harper. "Fine.

I'm assuming someone will tell me what my actual job is at some point?"

"Get through your session with Noah, then find me. I'll point you in the right direction."

He nodded, but she was already out the door, heading down the hall, her sneakers squeaking every third step on the stained linoleum.

He thought about waiting for Noah right there, but Harper might come back. So he headed out, looking for another safe place to hide. He hated being without a weapon. Without his left hand. The vulnerability never left these days, and he wondered if it ever would.

The blue hallway led past four different exam rooms, three of which were occupied, the doors closed. The fourth was empty and Seth walked in. There was one poster about STDs and another about HIV, both with stern warnings about always using a condom. Seth's hand went automatically to his back pocket where he kept his handy Trojans, two at the ready no matter what. The moment of optimism fizzled as he moved his left arm, the weight of the prosthetic reminding him again that his days as a chick magnet were over. Not that he'd actually been one, but the uniform, when he'd worn one, had helped. Being with Nate helped even more. There were always women around Nate who needed comfort after being passed over.

He looked at the plastic again—five fingers, finger-nails, little hairs on the knuckles, veins. No matter how masterfully the plastic was molded, it was still fake. Like a mannequin's hand, like a G.I. Joe. He fought the urge to smash the damn thing into the wall.

"What can I help you with today?"

Seth spun at the feminine voice to find a doctor standing in the doorway. She was reading an open file and chewing on the end of a pencil. She looked young, as if she'd just gotten out of medical school and her long, curly brown hair was pulled back in a messy ponytail. When she looked up at him, he looked down, giving her a good view of his baseball cap but not his face.

"I'm not a patient," he said, darting a quick glance. She was pretty. Especially her eyes.

Her gaze went right to his fake arm. "No?"

He flushed hotly. "I'm new here. I'm an aide."

"That's great," she said. She put the file back in a pocket on the inside of the door. "I'm Karen. Dr. Eckhardt. I was the new kid, until you."

"Nice to meet you."

She moved over to the exam table and leaned against it, trim in her blue scrubs, looking him over from bottom to top.

He needed to get the hell out of here, but he couldn't just run. Instead he turned his side to her as he feigned interest in the supplies on the shelf. Tongue depressors, cotton balls… Yeah, this was a clever ploy. He should have just stayed in Harper's office. What the hell was wrong with him?

"I didn't know we'd found someone new. What brings you to the clinic?"

"I'm just here to lend a hand."

"No pun intended?"

He wasn't at all sure how to take that. Another quick

glance found her smiling. He didn't think she was making fun of him, so he smiled as he stepped toward the door. "Right."

"Well, I think it's great. We can use all the help we can get."

Two women in scrubs were heading down the hall, so he stopped. "What about you?"

"Me? I switch-hit—I get paid for working at Kaiser Permanente, at the Sunset Hospital, but I spend a lot of time volunteering here."

"Why here?"

"Someone needs to do it."

"That's it, huh?"

"Well, to be honest, my attending physician looks kindly on those who give back to the community."

"I see."

"So what am I supposed to call you?"

"Seth'll do."

"Okay, Seth'll Do. Glad to have you on board."

The hall was clear, so he headed out, glancing back just as he reached the hallway. Her gaze had moved down to his ass. It surprised him. Maybe he wasn't a total turnoff. Then again, she did like charity work.

One of the exam room doors opened, so he slipped around the corner. An older Hispanic man and a middle-aged black woman sat behind a Plexiglas barrier in a large room overrun with files. Four phones, all of which were either ringing or blinking, were within arm's reach, as were two old computers.

Outside that office was the waiting room. There were

over a dozen people, three of whom were little kids, sitting in the ugly plastic chairs. He frowned seeing how many of the adults looked strung out and dangerous. Harper had warned him about the patient load here, but for some reason he hadn't expected kids. Mostly that's why the poor went to the doctor.

He leaned against the wall to watch. Surveillance. At least he could still do a visual. Of course, if something went wrong—say, someone should happen to recognize him—he couldn't do a thing about it except perhaps throw his fake hand at them. It might freak them out long enough for him to run like hell.

His gaze went down again, to the weight at the end of his arm. He'd never get used to it. He'd had to carry heavy crap for years, sixty-pound packs through unrelenting heat and treacherous terrain. Nothing had ever felt this unwieldy.

And, of course, there was that incredibly annoying phantom pain. He'd heard about that, read about it even, but it was one of those things that had to be experienced. Kind of like being shot at. If it hadn't happened to you, you didn't know shit.

If the fake hand were more useful, he might have accepted the whole thing more readily. But all it did was squeeze and open. That's it. And even though it was electric, he still had to move his shoulder to get it to do that.

When he saw Noah, he was gonna ask him for a hook. It had to be better than this. He might be able to do something with a hook. Hurt someone. Protect himself. And, besides, it would look a hell of a lot cooler than the mannequin hand.

A kid started crying in the waiting room, but the mother didn't seem to notice. Seth didn't know what she was on, but it was probably heroin, not meth, given her lethargy. Besides, she didn't look like a meth addict. She still had reasonably nice skin and hair, although she could have used a bath.

The kid, who must have been about two, had dropped something underneath the table and he couldn't reach it. The more he tried, the louder he screamed. Finally a little girl, older than the screamer but not by much, came to the rescue. Not one of the adults had even batted an eye.

It was a tough world all over. For kids, for addicts, for soldiers. And so what? None of it meant anything. Not a damn thing. He turned around. The coast was clear, so he headed back to his appointment, feeling as drained and tired as if he'd actually done something.

HARPER WALKED INTO her office as quietly as she could. She wanted to watch as Noah applied the facial prosthetics, but she didn't want to make Seth more self-conscious than he already was.

Noah stood, while Seth sat in her chair with the desk lamp pointed at his face. A large toolbox was open, and inside she saw pieces of flesh-colored silicone and latex, paintbrushes and small bottles. Of more interest was Seth. He sat perfectly still, back tall, head straight, like the soldier he was. Noah was smoothing his chin with a paintbrush. When he stepped away, Harper could see the difference in Seth's face. It was, indeed, subtle. But would she be able to swear it was the man on the poster? Maybe. But then, Noah wasn't finished.

She continued to watch as the painstaking process went on. And on. Every time she thought he had to be finished with the chin, he did something else with it. Shading, painting, until she would swear it was all Seth. Finally Noah gave an approving nod.

"Take a break," he said, his voice quiet and deep. "The nose will take longer."

Seth's head bowed for a long moment. Before looking up, he said, "You gonna stand there the rest of the day?"

"I might," she said. "It is my office."

Noah turned. "How are you, Dr. Douglas?"

"Harper," she said, holding out her hand as she walked into the room. "I'm fine. Man, you do great work."

He smiled as softly as he spoke. But that was all that was soft about him. She'd learned about his past in bits and pieces, mostly from other doctors. How agents in the field would refuse dangerous assignments unless Noah was the man in charge of their disguise. How he'd been offered everything and the moon to work in Kuwait. And, finally, how he'd given it all up to work with people who'd been broken either by disease, accident or at birth. He built faces that had been destroyed by fire. He brought humanity back to those who needed it the most.

"I do my best," he said. "But right now I need to go wash out my brushes."

When he left, Seth stood up and walked over to the

small mirror on her left wall. He examined his face, skimming the fake part of his chin. "Shit."

"I told you. You'll be just different enough."

"We could have used him in Delta Force."

"I think he's had enough of fighting and wars."

"He told me he works only on medical cases now."

"Yep. That's how I met him. He came here to help a little girl who'd been burned in an apartment fire."

Seth cursed, then turned to face her. She found herself looking at his eyes. This had been a good idea, this whole work thing. He looked more alive than he had in ages.

"I have to get going," she said. "I just wanted to check up on you. Make sure everything was okay."

He nodded. "I've asked him to take the hand back. I've decided to go with a hook."

She waggled her eyebrows. "Ooh, neat. Gonna get a peg leg, too?"

"Very amusing."

"No, I think a hook's a good idea. You'll get a lot of use out of that."

"Still won't be able to hold my dick with it, though."

She smiled. "You say that now, but just wait. Where there's a will…"

"Go to work, Harper."

She nodded. "Introduce yourself to me when you're done. I'm not sure I'll recognize you."

"I'll be the guy with one hand."

She went to the door. "Hey, I know—you can clap for me, and then we'll finally know the answer."

His curse followed her down the hall. Yep, this had been a damn good idea.

NATE PRATCHETT STOOD at the door of the abandoned apartment building, huddled in his jacket as he waited for Kate. It was her first time at that place, and he wanted to make sure she became familiar with the area. She was checking the back of the building, making sure they were alone. He'd already given the front a once-over. The only people he'd ever seen here were the homeless seeking shelter, but this place wasn't a top pick even for them. Most of the walls were destroyed or rotted to the point of crumbling. Inside, it was drafty and the stench of mold overpowered.

He heard a crack, a stick broken by a footfall, and he pulled out his weapon even though he knew it had to be Kate.

It was. He was glad to see she had her weapon pointed at him. Better safe than sorry.

He nodded at her and they entered the building together. The stink hit hard, but it didn't stop them from walking through the wreckage in the middle of the worst of East Los Angeles, until they hit what was once someone's bedroom. Nate put down the bag he'd brought from home, opened the closet door. He glanced at Kate, who'd naturally expected to see a closet, not a dresser. He pushed the furniture back with ease, since it was just an empty shell. It hit the wall of the closet only to reveal a large hole in the floor. Propped against the rim was a ladder which would lead them down to a very large room below.

The place used to be the home of a particularly violent Colombian gang whose members had been deported or killed two years ago. He'd found out about this place from an old friend who dealt in weapons, one who'd already sold off everything of value by the time he hooked up with Nate. But Nate's concern wasn't weapons, it was the concealed nature of the place itself. And the size. There was water, heat, even a shower below, and no one the wiser above.

He sent Kate down first. He saw her shudder as she began the descent and he didn't blame her. But then he thought about what was down there and he knew these precautions were necessary. He only hoped they were enough.

It was his turn to get the bag and climb down, pulling the cord on the back of the door to close it behind them. Then it was the kind of dark that stole a man's senses. The only reality the ladder in his grip, the rungs underfoot.

Kate's gasp told him she'd found the bottom. He hurried, and when he'd reached her side she whispered, "Tell me again why we can't use the flashlight?"

"It'll be light soon enough. Close your eyes or the light will blind you."

"Blind me?"

"Temporarily." He heeded his own advice, but the light when he swung the door open hurt even through his closed lids. He waited until the pain was gone, then he opened his eyes. His gaze turned immediately to Kate.

Her eyes grew wide, but not from the lighting. She gawked at the size of the room, at the equipment lining the walls. It was a laboratory, as well stocked as any major drug-company lab. But there was only one drug being studied here—an antidote to the most horrible death he could imagine.

"Well, it's about time you got here."

Nate spun at the voice behind him. "Tam," he whispered as the sight of her knocked the wind straight out of his lungs. Dammit, it got worse every visit. She just kept getting more beautiful.

3

ONE WEEK FROM THE day Seth started working at the clinic, Harper realized it had been a really bad idea. Although each morning he dutifully put on his face mask, as he liked to call the three pieces of painted silicone that changed his features just enough, by the time he got to work, he was in such a foul mood that no one dared get close enough to recognize him. Yes, she understood that it was difficult for him. And, yes, he should have been out saving the world instead of cleaning up puke. But still. He was scaring the patients. And the doctors. All except Karen.

Every time Harper saw the two of them together, at least one of them was smiling. Mostly Karen, but sometimes Seth, so what the hell was that about? The last time he'd smiled in the house was…well, not recently.

They drove home together, and while it only lasted about ten minutes, it could be pretty tense. Then Seth would hit the shower, change into clean jeans and a T-shirt no matter that it was usually freezing because she didn't want to heat an empty house, then head down to the basement. She'd pretty much given up on asking him if he wanted to join her for dinner.

Sometimes, just for spite, she hid the cheese so he couldn't make his damn sandwiches. He just ate peanut butter and jelly. Some meal for a man trying to heal.

But the truly weird thing was the looks he gave her. No, it wasn't looks, it was just the one.

She refocused on the chart in front of her. The patient was twenty-two years old, a young woman who was bright, confident and had the whole world at her feet. And she was HIV-positive. Her ex-boyfriend didn't like condoms. Of course, the girl hadn't known then that he was a cheating bastard. Instead she'd thought he was just like the great-looking guys in the movies, in the magazines. How could a hunk like him catch a disease? That didn't happen, right?

Harper wrote the scrips for the appropriate drug cocktail, hoping this girl would be one of the lucky ones.

Then came the next chart and the next, and when she finally looked around her office, it was almost seven. She usually left around six, so how come Seth hadn't come by to see where she was?

She stood and stretched her neck and back, wishing she could justify the expense of a massage, but her wages here were laughable. Which was okay, she supposed, because a doctor in this town couldn't get more low-profile. The good part about working at the clinic was her hours with patients. The bad part was writing all the grants and the fund-raising to keep the place going. Combining the two kept her busy. Kept her from thinking about the mess she was in. For the most part, at least.

She put her stethoscope in her top drawer, then

headed for the doctors' lounge, which was more like a big closet with chairs and a coffeemaker than a lounge one would find at a private clinic. But Seth wasn't there. After a quick chat with one of the volunteer doctors, she checked out the reception desk, the offices, the supply room. He was nowhere to be found and no one had seen him.

Karen had probably taken him home. Harper couldn't imagine Seth being so stupid as to take her to their house, so it had to be Karen's. But he was wearing the latex on his face, which would surely come off when they got down to it.

Goddamn him. What kind of a bonehead would let sex endanger his very life? The lives of all of them? Yeah, it had been a while, but so what? She wasn't getting any either, and he didn't see her lifting her skirt for the first decent pair of trousers to walk by. Karen wasn't even that great a physician. So she'd smiled at him, big deal. Who wouldn't? He was a really great-looking man. Especially now, with his hair down around his collar. A woman would have to be blind not to notice his muscles. Every time he mopped the floors, Harper caught some woman staring at his back. Or his butt.

On the other hand, maybe getting laid was just what he needed. Let him get his aggressions out on Karen. Then maybe he'd stop being such a pain.

She headed back to her office, her thoughts stubbornly staying on Seth and his muscles, despite three attempts to stop it. He was like a bad song in her head, playing over and over. No, he was more of a sore tooth. Yeah, Seth the toothache.

The thought made her grin, but that froze on her face the second she stepped into her office. Seth hadn't gone home with Karen after all. He was standing by her filing cabinet, glaring her way.

"Where've you been?"

"Me?" she asked. "I've been looking for you."

"I had to take the trash out back. I thought…"

"That I'd gone home without you? Don't be silly."

He tugged his baseball cap lower down his forehead. "Fine. I'll wait in the car."

"Don't bother, I'm ready. I just need my purse." She hurried by him, pissed that he was pissed. Embarrassed that she'd gone straight to the gutter. Besides, he wouldn't sleep with Karen. He liked being miserable too much.

She got her keys out as she walked by him again, and her shoulder brushed his. Brushed, not hit, but he stepped back, his mouth open, his eyes big. It hadn't even been his left arm. "Come on," she said. "I couldn't have hurt you."

His face turned crimson and he practically ran out of the office. She stood there for a moment, trying to figure out what had happened. She must have done something to set him off, but hell if she knew what. It was worse than dealing with a teenager. And, frankly, she had too many real concerns to worry about Seth's weirdness.

CORKY BAKER HAD A problem, and from what he could see, it wasn't going away anytime soon. Sitting in the traffic jam known as the 405 gave him too much time to think. To worry. Ever since he'd listened to Vince Yarrow and Nate Pratchett, he'd been hip-deep in lies, some so outrageous that only the government itself had the balls to go there.

He wondered for the hundredth time what the hell he was doing. He loved his job at the *L.A. Times*. He loved being an investigative journalist. He just wasn't crazy about being a walking target. The more he found out about Omicron, the clearer it became that there was, in fact, a conspiracy. Could he prove it? Not yet. But he would. If, that is, he lived long enough.

He'd become almost as paranoid as Vince and his friends. His notes were coded, with copies in his safe-deposit box. He kept his associates and his editors pretty much in the dark. He'd sent his wife and son out of the state, although he was beginning to think that wasn't far enough.

A smart man would leave it alone. Hell, he'd done more than he should have by exposing the cache of nerve gas in the paper and on national television. It sure hadn't taken Omicron long to turn that around. Senator Raines had stepped right up to the plate and named the Delta Force men as the people responsible. The official story had holes all over it, but he couldn't get a soul to go on the record. Nobody wanted to touch this, not in the military, not in Washington. They all ducked when they saw him coming. Not that he wasn't used to that, but these people, all of them connected in some way to Omicron and the CIA, had let him know in not-so-subtle ways that if he continued to poke around there would be consequences.

Well, screw them. Corky Baker might not believe in much, but he did believe in a free press.

He advanced another few feet on the freeway, then stopped again. Reaching over to the passenger seat, he grabbed the small tape recorder he kept there. Without looking, he hit Record. "Tell Eli to come to the house in the morning to talk about the interview with George Page." He clicked the machine off, then on again as he thought of one more thing. "Ask N about the lead chemist in Kosovo."

This time he put the tape recorder back on the seat. He inched his way along the freeway as his thoughts turned to Pulitzer prizes and big damn paychecks. All he had to do was stay alive. Shouldn't be all that hard. He was a public figure. People would ask too many questions. He'd live, and those Omicron bastards would go down in flames. In fact, he'd be the one to light the first match.

SETH WAITED UNTIL Harper was done in the kitchen before he made his ham-and-cheese sandwich. Not only did he not want her to see how much trouble he had with the knife, with the mayonnaise, with every goddamn thing in the kitchen, but being anywhere near her was getting more and more difficult.

It wasn't just his dreams anymore. The woman haunted him in the daytime now, too. Even when she was in the next room, in the same room, his thoughts went places they had no business going.

He'd tried to talk himself out of it. He had a million reasons not to want her, but his body wouldn't listen. He didn't even have the excuse that she was the only woman around. Not anymore. It was even conceivable that the other doctor, Karen, was interested in him. Probably for the novelty of sleeping with a cripple. But what did he care? He should go for it. Ask her out. It wasn't natural for a man to go this long without sex. No wonder he was going insane.

He got two pieces of whole-wheat out of the bag, then did up the twist tie with his teeth. The mayo jar went under his left arm to hold it steady while he unscrewed the cap. Then he had to put the cap down, take the jar in his right hand and put that down. Get the knife, shove the bread up next to the plate so it would stay steady, then spread each side slowly and carefully. Once that was done, he went through the whole under-the-arm procedure again just to close the damn thing.

It all took too long and felt too awkward, and he didn't see how he could go through the rest of his life like this.

To add injury to insult, his hand hurt like hell. The left one. He knew it wasn't there, but still, it hurt. A lot. All he wanted to do was rub it, right in the center of his palm. If he could do that, it would be fine—the cramp, if that's what it was, would be gone and he would stop thinking about it—but there was no hand to rub. It was just a pain that followed him around like a shadow. Oh, sometimes it itched in addition to the ache, and that was even worse. Harper said it would get better as time went on. Which was fine except every single day felt like it went on forever, so when, exactly, were things going to improve?

It probably would have been okay if it was the only pain he couldn't assuage. But there was this other thing, this hormonal thing that was probably a result of the amputation, although no one talked about it. It had to be some kind of chemical misfire that made him want her like this. As if he couldn't breathe until he was inside her. As if she was the magic that would take his pain away.

He opened the pack of honey-baked ham with his teeth, then slipped out a few slices. Good thing he had teeth or he'd have been up the creek. Now if he could only figure out a convenient way to unzip his fly....

"I'm having some ice cream. Oh, you're not done."

He spun around, and the plastic bag of ham went flying out of his mouth. It hit the floor and slid, half the ham spilling on the linoleum as it went. Instantly he was so angry he could barely see, his eyes blurred behind a veil of red mist.

The only thing that penetrated was her laughter.

His fist curled into a ball so tight he could feel his short fingernails cut into his palm. His heart beat fast, pounding against his ribs. And Harper thought it was hilarious.

He wanted to hurt her. To grab her by her shoulders and shake her. She had no right. No business. She was a doctor, for God's sake. She should know. But she didn't. She didn't understand, and that wasn't fair because it was all her fault. She'd stolen his hand, taken it from him when he was too weak to stop her. *Bitch.* She'd ripped him apart, and her laughter sounded like a Klaxon in the quiet old house, bouncing off the high ceiling and the big plate-glass windows. Christ, he was so angry he couldn't see. And he was getting hard at her laughter. What the hell was happening to him?

"Oh, God, I'm sorry. I shouldn't laugh. But, really, it was perfect."

He needed to get out, to go down to his basement, but she was standing in the way. He didn't dare touch her. He wasn't sure what he would do—hurt her or kiss her or…

"Come on, Seth. Where's your sense of humor? Even you have to see that was funny."

He saw no such thing. Not when she was in her robe. The material tight against her breasts, curved into her waist. The hollow at the base of her neck pale and delicate. He could imagine the smell of her, the clean womanly scent that made him ache every time she came close.

She walked toward him and he stiffened, panic constricting his throat. He had to get out, to leave before it got even worse, but he couldn't pass her. So he turned away, forced himself to walk to the front door. Then he was outside and the cold wind slapped him in the face.

He went down the six stairs to the crumbling walkway and the torn sidewalk. He went left, no reason. He walked on unsteady legs and kept walking until he got his feet under him and then he walked until the thickness in his pants went away. But the ache, the wound where he wanted her like air, wouldn't leave him. Not for blocks or miles.

HARPER GAVE UP WAITING for him an hour after he'd stormed out. She'd been a moron, which wasn't like her. Of course he'd been humiliated by the whole thing. He hated it when she walked in on him making his sandwich. Hated her to see him struggle. And she'd laughed.

It wouldn't surprise her in the least if he didn't come back at all. He'd probably rather sleep in a cardboard box than face her again.

She left the front window and headed to the kitchen, where she put her old kettle on the stove. What she really wanted was a good stiff drink, but she'd settle for tea. If she didn't have to work tomorrow… But she did. And so did Seth, so wherever he was, he needed to get his act together before seven.

This was not working out the way she'd hoped. She had to smile at the understatement. When she thought about how he'd looked at her…she wasn't sure if he'd wanted to kill her or take her to bed.

It was that look of his, the one that had confused her for months, only about a hundred times stronger.

What was it with him? She got out her tea collection and went for the chamomile. That and the nice clover honey would at least cut the chill from her bones.

He hadn't even grabbed his coat. So he was out there without his prosthetic, wearing nothing more than a T-shirt and jeans. If he had the brains God gave a post, he'd at least find himself a nice, warm bar.

She waited until the kettle sang, then poured herself a mug, which she took over to the kitchen table. Curling her leg underneath her, she sipped the hot tea, then

pulled the phone close. It took her a minute to remember
the number, but it was there, memorized out of neces-
sity. She dialed, and after five rings Kate answered.

"Hi," Harper said, wishing there was another way.
"Do you think you could take Seth for a while?"

NATE WATCHED TAMARA as she peered over her half-
glasses, reading test results from her latest run on the
antidote. He supposed he could have brought Kate with
him again on this supply run, but selfishly he wanted to
spend time with Tam alone.

She was close, damn close. She'd managed to take
most of the notes from the lab in Serbia when they'd
escaped and use them to recreate the serum, but what
she hadn't gotten was a method of dispensing the
antidote that would work effectively. Right now the
only way to be safe was to have the serum injected, but
that wouldn't work if the gas were let loose in the center
of a big factory or over an entire village. So she continued to work, alone, in the underground lab that was too
cold and too impersonal to be anything but a prison.

"Come out to dinner with me," he said.

She took off her glasses and stared at him in disbelief. God, her eyes were great. Slightly Asian, they were
full of intelligence and innocence at the same time.
"Have you been sniffing the vials again?"

He jumped down from the counter and walked closer
to her, close enough to see the little tendrils of dark hair
that had come loose from her tight ponytail. She was in
jeans, T-shirt and lab coat, but even the coat and the

glasses wouldn't convince a stranger that she was a brilliant chemist.

He'd be the first to admit that he hadn't been around many scientists in his life. His line of work lent itself more toward dictators and mercenaries. But he knew that Tam was not someone he'd have picked to be the brains of the operation. Like most sexist-pig men, he'd have pegged her as the saucy secretary or the babe on the payroll because she'd slept with the boss.

She'd disabused him of that notion the day they'd met.

"I'm not sniffing anything. You've been cooped up down here for too long. You need to get out. Have a beer. Laugh a little."

"I'm too close, Nate. I'm not going to take any chances now."

"I'm not asking you if you want to fly to Paris, Tam. Dinner. Even you have to eat."

"I eat just fine."

"MREs. Frozen dinners. That's no way to live."

"I'll live when I have the disbursement system ready to go."

He wanted to argue, but it was useless. She was an incredibly stubborn woman, and since he'd known her, she'd gotten her way in every single dispute. Except for that first one. She'd wanted to stay, convinced the government would be crazy to destroy the only hopes of an antidote to the nerve gas. In truth, it hadn't been him who'd persuaded her. The first bomb had done that.

"How come Kate didn't come with you?"

"She's working on the ledgers from Kosovo. It's

coming along, but slowly. She can only work on it at night. She's got that waitress gig at the IHOP."

Tam put down her clipboard and leaned against a large cabinet full of test results. "She likes this cop Vince, huh?"

"He's a good guy. He's been a real help since Seth was shot."

"How is Seth?"

Nate rubbed his chin, feeling the stubble of another ten-hour workday. "Physically he's improving, but he's still in a major depression."

"That's only to be expected."

"It's still tough. The guy's been in the service since he got out of college. And he was in the ROTC before that. All he knows is fighting."

"They're doing amazing things with prosthetics now. In a few years, he'll be able to do almost anything he could with his real hand. He just needs to be patient."

"Patient? Seth? Not gonna happen."

"He has no choice, though, does he?"

"You're right about that. I just feel bad for the guy."

"I feel bad for all of us." Her head went down and she sighed loudly. "I'm so tired. I just want my life back, you know? I want to go to a movie. I want to sleep late and go on dates and shop for shoes. But every time I try to slack off, this major wave of guilt hits me. What if they use the weapon today? What if a village is massacred while I'm watching TV?"

"You can only do what you can do. One step at a time. But it's important for you to take some breaks. This pace is going to kill you."

"I exercise on the treadmill. I take vitamins. I'm fine."

"You're pale as a ghost. You need to get outside more."

"It's almost ten o'clock."

"I wasn't just talking about tonight."

"Soon. I promise." She sighed.

"Do you need anything else?"

"A team of graduate students would be nice."

"Anything I can get you?"

"No," she said, smiling just a bit.

"That's a good look on you."

She frowned, looking down at her lab coat. "This?"

"The smile."

"Sweet but unnecessary. I'm fine. I'm not going completely nuts yet. And, as I've mentioned, I'm close."

He nodded, getting the hint. "Fine. I'm out of here. But don't be surprised to see me Friday."

"I'll have to remember to look at a calendar."

"Do that." He touched her shoulder and gave it a gentle squeeze. "It's not all going to go to hell if you have a nice dinner."

"Sweet man, it's already gone to hell."

He couldn't argue with that.

4

HARPER HUNG UP THE phone, but she didn't move. It was late, she should go to sleep. Tomorrow was a long day and she had to meet with the accountant, which made it even worse. But she hadn't heard Seth come back yet, and that worried her.

There was no question that he needed counseling. But he was such an incredibly stubborn fool that he wouldn't hear of it. Stupid, stupid. Now that Kate had turned her down, what was she supposed to do? Throw him out on the street? The man was wanted, and if those pricks from Omicron found him, they wouldn't kill him fast.

She leaned back in her chair, cursing yet again the day she'd gotten involved in this mess. The dreams about Serbia were a nightly affair now. It didn't matter how late she went to bed, what she ate or drank, how exhausted she was. She kept finding herself back among the dead.

What would it take to purge herself of these memories? Of the smells that filled her nostrils from thousands of miles and years away? Her head told her she wouldn't be free until Omicron was exposed, but her gut told her it was worse than that. She'd broken her cardinal rule: don't get involved.

Shit. She should have walked away and never looked back. Kept her eyes on her work and nothing more.

Where the hell was he? She couldn't even call the police to report him missing, now, could she? It ticked her off that she was even thinking about Seth. He was gone? Good. Let him stay gone. He was nothing but trouble.

Harper got up and headed toward her bedroom. It felt good to have her home as her own once more, even though it really wasn't *her* home. Nate had found this place and he'd wanted it because of the basement. Having a trauma room at the ready was fine for the rest of them, but for her it was a sword of Damocles. For the first six months she'd awakened at every noise, at every creak, certain she would end up watching over someone's death just before the place was raided and she was killed.

Great way to live.

The only thing that had gotten her through it was her work at the clinic. Nate had objected, of course, but she'd told him just where he could go. The job had become her world. She'd kept a nice distance from the staff, but she'd put her all into each patient. That she had to do administrative tasks was bearable as long as she got in her treatment hours.

That's when it all made sense. When she was helping people. Healing. Everything else in her life might have gone down the toilet, but at the clinic she gave hope, care, medicine, guidance. Nothing was better than that. She had a reason. A purpose.

She got ready for bed, taking her time in the bathroom as she gave her face a good cleansing and a minty mask. In the bedroom, she fluffed her pillows and pulled up her comforter. The room itself was spare—she hadn't spent much on decorating. Now, as she looked around the place, she wished she'd at least picked up some vases, put some fresh flowers on the counters or by her bed.

By the time she'd gotten the chill out of her feet and read a few chapters in a book she might never have time to finish, it was past midnight. Still Seth hadn't returned. She wondered if he'd been arrested. Or shot.

She turned out the light, determined to fall asleep immediately, curious if Seth's absence would give her a dreamless night. She hoped so.

SETH STOOD BY THE pay phone in front of the twenty-four-hour supermarket. It was late as hell, and he was so cold he could barely feel his fingers, but he didn't want to go back, not yet.

It wasn't that he didn't have the number or the correct change. It was that he had no idea what he was going to say.

His parents had thought he was dead. They'd had a funeral for their only son, and he knew that they had died a little themselves to have watched his casket lowered into the ground.

Now they knew he was alive. Not by hearing the words from their son's mouth but from watching a U.S. senator denounce him as a traitor to his country. Seth couldn't even imagine the pain his folks had gone through and the questions they must have.

It killed him to know he couldn't just take off for Seattle and talk to them, explain that he wasn't a criminal and that he hadn't disgraced them.

He thought about his little sisters. They weren't so little anymore, but he'd always see them as the two brats who followed him everywhere, who cried each time he had to leave for assignments that were shrouded in mystery.

His family, who'd stood behind him no matter what, had gone through hell the last couple of years. What was he going to say on this goddamn public phone that would make things better? Even more of a concern was that Omicron might have his parent's phone bugged.

He thought about what had happened to Christie. She'd thought—they'd all thought—that Nate was dead. She was Nate's only sister, and his death had been hard on her. Of course, she'd never suspected anything like Omicron when someone began stalking her. She'd just gotten frantic as the stalker had gotten closer and closer, and then Boone had gone to help. Together, they'd discovered that it wasn't just a stalker. It was Omicron, convinced that Nate was alive, sure that if they made Christie desperate enough, she'd reveal Nate's whereabouts.

They'd caught the guy directly responsible for stalking her and a few other hit men, but Christie couldn't go back to her old life. Like him, like all of them, she was on the run—and would be until Omicron was exposed. The only bright spot had been that she and Boone had become a couple. At least Boone had someone who wouldn't laugh at him.

Which wasn't the point. His first concern had to be his family's welfare. There was no choice, so he turned away from the phone, not willing to take the risk. He'd thought about writing to them, but he wasn't sure who was watching them. He'd put nothing past Omicron.

He should go back to the house. Harper would be in bed by now, so he wouldn't have to face her. He wasn't nearly as embarrassed about the ham as he was about running out like a five-year-old.

He shook his head as he headed back down the long street filled with cramped shops. Boyle Heights was an old Los Angeles neighborhood that had gone through a number of transitions. Mary Lee at the clinic had told him that in the forties and fifties it was a haven for Jewish immigrants. Signs of their tenure were still around: an old synagogue converted into an apartment building with the Hebrew letters still outlined on the brick, a secondhand resale shop with a kosher chicken on the window. But now Boyle Heights, like most inner-city neighborhoods, was ruled by the gangs. There was graffiti and tags on every available surface. Bloods, Crips, gangs he'd never heard of—they were all visible in brilliant spray-paint hues.

No one had bothered him on his walk. He'd passed plenty of guys wearing colors, but they'd caught sight of his stump and steered clear. Guess it was good for something.

Of course, they might have been avoiding him

because it was thirty degrees out here and he was wearing a T-shirt, jeans and no coat.

His gaze moved to the few feet in front of him as he neared the old house on St. Louis Street. Most of the people who lived in the area knew she was one of the doctors at the free clinic and therefore she was okay. He rode in on her ticket, which probably protected him more than his long hair or his disguise.

When he got to Harper's, he thought again about not going in. He hated having to come here, having to do the crap work at the clinic. He hated everything about his life now, not the least of which was being a fugitive. The worst of it was feeling so helpless.

He wondered what Nate was doing tonight. Whatever it was, he was furthering their cause. Probably with Kate or Vince at his side, watching his back.

There was nothing for him to do but go on inside. To crawl into the basement and dream of days when he'd been whole. When he hadn't given Harper a second thought.

He reached across his body to his left pocket and took out his key. The front light was on, so it wasn't a problem, but the house was wired with some of the most sophisticated alarms in the world. Luckily he'd been the one who'd installed them when they'd bought the house, so he knew exactly how to get in quietly.

The moment he stepped inside, he knew Harper was asleep. Yeah, she could have just been in bed, but there was a different energy in the house when she was awake. He'd never say those words out loud, knowing how crazy he sounded. Shit, his unit would have laughed him out of Delta. Even so, he knew what he knew, and Harper was sleeping.

Another thing he knew how to do was be quiet. He'd had a lot of training in that department. He'd been on a hell of a lot of missions where to fail was to die. So he didn't make much noise. Not even when he went down the long hallway to Harper's bedroom, not when he stood in front of her door wondering what in hell he expected to find. He wasn't about to knock. And he might be a lot of things, but he wasn't about to go in uninvited. Not that she ever would. Not him. Not ever.

He turned before he did something stupid, but instead of heading to bed, he went to the bathroom. The chill had gone deep and he needed a good long, hot shower.

Once there, he stripped, turned on the water and avoided looking at himself in the mirror. With the room steamed sufficiently, he got under the flow, wincing at the heat. But he toughed it out until his whole body felt warm and relaxed. He hadn't realized just how exhausted he was. The thought of going down to that cold, sterile basement, with the oversized OR lights and hulking machines all around his bed, was enough to make him wish he hadn't come back at all.

Like the good soldier he used to be, he grabbed his washcloth off the rod, then picked up the soap with it. That's how he washed these days. With the soap wrapped in terry. The only thing he hadn't figured out was how to scrub his right shoulder. A back scrubber helped, but there were just some parts he couldn't get to.

Even more disconcerting to him was washing his

hair with one hand. He had no problem cleaning his hair, but it felt wrong. Weird how some things felt worse than others. Like those slip-on shoes. He hated those with a vengeance.

Finally he was as clean as he could get and warm all the way through, so he turned off the shower. He dried as much as possible and picked up his jeans. But he couldn't put them back on. Instead he wrapped the towel around his waist, using the side of the sink as a hand substitute.

He shoved his clothes under his arm and headed out into the chilly hallway—and right into Harper.

She gasped. He dropped his clothes, and the knot of his towel loosened. He caught it about a second too late.

"Oh, God, I'm sorry," she said. She didn't have on her robe. Just a sleep shirt that draped over her breasts, molding her nipples.

"What the hell are you doing?"

She stepped back abruptly. "Well, excuse me for worrying."

"What, you think now that I'm a cripple, I can't take care of myself?"

"No, I don't—"

Without picking up his clothes, he walked past her, bumping her shoulder, cutting her off. He couldn't look at her and he couldn't stand for her to see him like this. It didn't matter that she'd seen his stump a thousand times, that she'd given him the goddamn thing. He had to get out of there.

Halfway down to the basement his eyes started to

burn, which made him want to break down the door, destroy everything in his path. Instead he just went to the side of his bed, dropped his towel on the floor and put his hand on his swelling erection.

VINCE HAD A BAD feeling about this. He should have heard from Corky Baker this morning. When he'd called the reporter, there had been no answer. Not on the home phone, the cell phone. And no one at the *Times* had any information.

Ever since Vince had gotten involved in this Omicron mess, he'd learned to be extraordinarily cautious. Although he hadn't been in Kosovo, couldn't have found the place on a map, he was in this fight to the end. Because of Kate. Because if anything happened to her, he wasn't at all sure what he would do. She was the first—and last—woman he would ever love. And when it was over, when Omicron was exposed and Kate had her identity back, he planned on having one hell of a good life with her. Yeah. Just the two of them. So he'd be careful. Damn careful.

He'd had to wait until nightfall to come. Nate was pretty sure that Baker's house was under surveillance, so they had to be in full stealth mode.

Kate had wanted to come, but he'd made up some bullshit about needing Nate to break in when the truth was he just wanted to keep her out of danger. It wasn't possible, of course. Just knowing what she knew was enough to get her killed. But he didn't have to watch it happen.

He would never have believed meeting Kate would

have led him here. To quit his job as an LAPD homicide detective, to become part of this team of fugitives. Almost more unbelievable is that he'd had to go to Corky Baker and ask the reporter for help. He and Baker had a long, unhappy history of bumping into each other at murder scenes. Vince trying to solve them, Baker trying to earn Brownie points from his editor by snooping everywhere he didn't belong. That very trait made him the right man to get on Omicron's case.

Of course Vince had realized he was putting Baker in harm's way. But this was the big time, the real deal, and if Baker ever wanted a chance for a Pulitzer, this was it.

Which was why Vince was worried as hell that Baker hadn't checked in. He and Nate were dressed in black, like movie burglars, and they each had black ski masks to cover their pale white faces.

He felt stupid, as if this was all blown way out of proportion, even as the logical part of him knew the precautions weren't nearly enough.

Without a word, they got out of the truck and headed toward the house, but they went via backyards and, briefly, across an alley. It was a little tricky to pick out the right house, as Vince had only come through the front door before.

Once they'd scaled the fence, Vince knew he'd found the right place. What bothered him was that he couldn't remember if Baker had a dog. He remembered the kid, about eleven, cute, which meant he must have taken after his mom.

Nate pulled out a penlight, small but strong, and led

them past the swimming pool. It was covered over for the winter, and leaves from the nearby trees had settled on the plastic.

Before they even attempted to get in, Nate did his thing with the alarm system. Vince waited by the back door, trying to come up with a reason Baker wouldn't have called, but none of the excuses held water.

Vince would have told him to forget it if they hadn't needed him so badly. Truth be told, Baker was turning out to be damn good at his job. Go figure.

"The alarm's not on," Nate said quietly. "And it's not broken."

"Shit." Those bad feelings had been right on the money. Dammit. "Let's do this."

Despite what he'd told Kate, it was Vince himself who broke in. He had a nifty lock-pick set he'd gotten from a lifer he'd sent up three years ago. It took all of about ten seconds before the lock clicked and they were inside the dark, quiet house.

Once they'd closed the door, Nate got out a special little gadget that Vince had heard about but never seen. It was a monitor, the size of an iPod, that searched out video and audio signals. The little gizmo would alert them if there was a camera or a mike anywhere in the house. He watched intently as Nate pressed some buttons. It didn't take long for Nate to give the go-ahead.

Vince got his own flashlight out and led Nate past the big grand piano and the long glass coffee table until they were just outside Baker's office.

A light bled under the door.

Vince looked at Nate, who shut off his flashlight and undid the safety on his Glock. Following suit, Vince prepared himself for a fight.

He waited until his breathing evened, then he opened the door fast, rushing inside.

A kid he didn't recognize sat in Baker's swivel chair. He looked to be in his twenties and scared spitless.

At his feet, next to the small couch, lay Corky Baker in a pool of congealing blood.

Vince's stomach lurched and he thought he might puke. Not because he'd never seen a murder victim— hell, he'd been a homicide detective for years before he'd hooked up with Kate—but because Baker was dead because of Vince.

He'd always hated the bastard, but he'd turned to Baker with the Omicron story because he got the job done. Vince had known it was dangerous. He'd been there when Seth had had his hand blown off. But somehow seeing Baker in his own home, his office, cemented the reality in a way nothing had. In all likelihood, Vince was going to die, just like Baker. Kate would die, very possibly in front of his eyes. As would Nate, Harper and Seth.

Nate had the kid up and in a hammerlock when Vince looked up. "Who are you?" Nate asked, keeping his voice low and threatening.

"Eli Lieberman," the kid said, although it was hard to understand him what with the arm pressed against his vocal cords. "I work with Mr. Baker."

"Why'd you kill him?"

"I didn't." The kid was visibly shaking and his pale face grew pasty. "I was supposed to meet him at eight—"

Nate loosened his grip. Eli coughed, then started again. "I was supposed to help him transcribe some notes on an old case he'd worked on. But he didn't answer any of my calls. So I came over to see if he was okay."

"How did you get in?" Vince asked.

"The front door was open."

"Open as in ajar or just unlocked?"

"Ajar. I knew his wife and son were out of town. So I thought maybe Mr. Baker had fallen or…"

"What was the old case?"

"A triple homicide in Compton. It's coming up for trial and they've subpoenaed his records."

Still holding the kid by the neck, Nate holstered his weapon, then reached into the back pocket of Eli's jeans. He pulled out a wallet and tossed it to Vince.

The ID matched the name the kid had given, and so did the employee badge from the *L.A. Times*. Which probably didn't matter, because Vince believed him. There was still one big unanswered question. "Why didn't you call the police?"

"I thought about it, but—"

"But what?"

"I knew he'd been working on something big. Something that he was scared about. If I called the cops, they would have taken everything. All his notes. Only, I think that would be the last thing Mr. Baker would have wanted."

"So you've been going through his papers?"

Eli nodded.

"You know who we are?"

"I don't think you're with Omicron," he said. "I think they—" he nodded at Baker with closed eyes "—they did that."

Nate let him go and he stumbled forward a couple of steps. His hand went to his neck. "I think you're the one's who are supposed to have made that nerve gas."

"You don't believe we didn't?" Nate asked.

"Mr. Baker didn't. I don't know."

Vince walked over to the desk, to the strewn papers and small audiotapes. "This doesn't make sense. Why would they kill Baker and leave his notes?"

Eli's gaze moved to the floor by the bookcase.

Vince didn't understand until he moved over and saw the safe open. "How the hell did you know about that?"

"I've been Mr. Baker's assistant for the last six months. He'd told me he was doing something dangerous and that if something happened to him…"

"He gave you the combination?"

Eli dug under the papers on the desk and pulled out an envelope. It was addressed to Eli Lieberman and it gave his address. It even had a stamp. Inside, the letter was brief. Three sets of five numbers. Nothing else.

"What are the other numbers?"

"I don't know. I just kept trying until the safe opened."

Vince looked to Nate, who gave him a shrug, then turned to the kid. With his stomach queasy once more, he said, "These notes got your boss killed. Now that you've read them, you're on the list."

Two red splotches appeared on Eli's cheeks. He

wasn't a bad-looking guy, except that he was so damn skinny. He was tall, with dark hair and dark eyes. Definitely not a jock. "I don't think they should get away with this," he said, his voice tight and quivering.

"They already did," Nate said. "We'd better get out of here." He joined Vince at the desk and started picking up papers and tapes.

"You can't do that."

"We're already wanted," Nate said. "Adding tampering with a crime scene won't hurt."

"No, I mean I should."

Vince stopped. "You should what?"

"Take his notes. Go on from where he left off."

Vince smiled. "You don't need that in your life. What are you, twenty-five?"

"Twenty-three. I skipped some grades."

"You want to live to twenty-five? Get the hell out of here. And don't even think about Omicron. Ever."

Eli shook his head. "I understand it's dangerous. But I'm not just going to walk away. And, frankly, you're in no position to argue with me. I'm the only one who can decipher his notes. Besides, you need someone on the outside if you ever want to get out of this mess."

Vince turned to Nate, but he didn't expect to see the agreement on his face. "Are you kidding me? This kid?"

"This kid is all we've got."

"He won't last a day."

"I don't know," Nate said. "Omicron would probably think that, too. He might just be the perfect one for the job."

"I don't want his blood on my hands," Vince said,

lowering his voice, although he suspected Eli heard him just fine.

"I do believe that ship has sailed," Nate said. "They know he came into the house. And they know he didn't come out."

"Shit. You think they have the office wired?"

Nate shook his head. "I think we broke up the party early. But you know damn well they're watching."

Vince let that sink in. Then he turned to face young Eli. "Do you own a gun?"

Eli shook his head.

"You'd better get one."

5

NOAH HAD PRETTY MUCH taken over Harper's office with all his equipment. To Seth, it looked more like the man was there to repair a car than to fit him with a hook.

Despite having seen prosthetic hooks before, some part of Seth's psyche had fixed on a Captain Hook type deal, one that would look right at home in a pirate movie. Of course, the one Noah had on the table wasn't anything like that.

"Come on and take a look," Noah said, holding the metal claw with obvious pride. "This'll do more for your dexterity than anything else out there. And here's the cool thing—we put on this wrist here…." He lifted up what looked like a coupling device. "That's static, but the center piece can turn. You can adjust that according to the task."

He picked up the claw again, and Seth could see right away where it would fit into the wrist. "This is the basic model, although I've done a few things to make it right for you. You'll wear this for most of your daily tasks. It grips with the thumb and two fingers, and you adjust the strength of the grip by the muscles in your shoulder. It's great for picking up a piece of pipe or a mug or what have you. Doorknobs. Things like that.

"Brooms," Seth said. "Mops. Buckets."

"Yeah, sure," Noah said, not noticing his sarcasm, which was probably a good thing.

"But look here." The older man lifted a metal piece that was about the same size as the claw, only instead of the gripper there was a screwdriver. "There's quite a number of pieces that you can swap out for the hook. Silverware, for instance. All kinds of tools."

"I think I saw this stuff on *Inspector Gadget*."

"What's that?"

"A kids' TV show."

Noah nodded. "It wouldn't surprise me if this whole idea came from a cartoon. It's just that cool."

Seth laughed at the unexpected words. He was beginning to see why Noah had quit the CIA. He'd stick out there because he'd want to be his own man. Not that every CIA agent he'd met was like the goons from Omicron, but enough were to make him suspicious.

Way before Kosovo, his unit in Delta Force had had to deal with the Company. It was never a smooth union. Different styles, different objectives, even on the same missions.

"How long were you with the CIA?"

"Sixteen years."

"I hear you saved a lot of lives."

"Funny," Noah said. "That's what I heard about you. Now you want to try this contraption on or what?"

Seth nodded and sat down in the chair in front of

Noah. It was early, not quite seven, and knowing he was going to get the hook, Seth had come in to the clinic without his prosthetic hand. As awkward as the fake hand was, it made him even more uncomfortable to be without it. To have just the stump sticking out of his shirt. So much so that he'd made Harper wait while he ran back to the house to fetch the thing and put it in the car. Just in case.

Noah showed him how to put on the wrist, which was a more streamlined version of how he put on the hand. Then he attached the hook. A moment later, Seth moved the digits. It took all his concentration, but he did it. And he could already see how this claw was going to be a hell of a lot more useful. The only question he had was about the weight. It was heavy, and he'd have to wear it a lot to get his body used to it. In order to fight again, he had to get to the point where he didn't think about his body. That his weapon and his arms and his eyes all worked as a unit.

"It's gonna take some getting used to, but that's to be expected." Noah picked up his arm and studied the connection between man and metal. "It looks like a real good fit from here, but you let me know if you have any chafing or bruising. We can fix you right up."

"Those other gadgets," Seth asked. "Do they cost a lot?"

He nodded. "They don't come cheap. I'm gonna leave you with a couple of brochures. You see if there's anything that looks to be particularly useful. We'll see what we can do."

"Harper says you're not getting paid for this."

"I've been paid."

"What?"

"Don't worry about it. I know what you do and I know what you've lost."

Seth shook his head as he looked at his new claw. It was cooler. Made of titanium, it would last forever. And it was heavy enough to do some real damage should it come to that. "Thank you."

Noah was already packing up. "I was going to ask if you wanted to try some other models on, but I think this is the one."

"When will you be back?"

"If you need me, call. If not, I'll check up on you in about six months." He lifted a large box to the table in front of Seth. "Those are your facial pieces. I made you enough to last a while. You look like you're not having any trouble on that score, so we should be set."

Seth stood. He let his arm hang down loose against his body. It made him lean a bit to compensate, which he'd have to work on. But it was the right model. Which didn't mean he was going to be the way he was. It was still a poor substitute for flesh and blood. And yet he felt something in his chest. Hope? Nah. Well, maybe just a little.

HARPER WAS ANXIOUS to see Seth's new prosthesis, but she hadn't had a breather since she'd walked in the door. The flu was hitting the area hard, and the kids were stacked up in the waiting room. She wished there was more to be done to help them, but with the flu the best thing was to get the vaccine before you got sick. Most of the people who came here wouldn't even think of getting their children vaccinated, let alone themselves. The tragedy was that she'd had to send two babies to the hospital this morning, and it was fifty-fifty if they'd check out again.

She finished putting her notes on the chart for a seventeen-year-old who'd caught the bug from her little sister, then headed for the coffee room. As she stepped to the door, she heard Seth's voice, and something in his tone made her stop. He sounded as if he was smiling. Not that she had a lot of experience with that particular sound, but she recognized it nonetheless. A second later someone laughed. A woman. When she spoke, Harper realized it was Karen.

Stepping even closer to the door, she felt a little guilty for eavesdropping but too curious to stop.

"Come on. I've got a bunch of great movies on TiVo."

Harper stopped breathing to listen better.

"I don't know…."

"Pass me that, would you?"

Silence. Should she go in? Or would Karen keep pressing? Actually, Harper liked Karen. She was a good doctor. Or, rather, was becoming one. The clinic had been the best thing she could have done. Born and raised in privilege, Karen had little idea how most people lived, and when she'd first arrived she'd been pretty bitchy about it, not bothering to see the people behind the addictions and the poverty. But in the last few months she'd really come around. She'd even gone to a couple of the street fairs where the clinic set up a booth to hand out condoms and educational material.

"I'm a really good cook," Karen said, her voice lower and more provocative. "Seriously. I went to a culinary school in Napa for a whole summer."

"Culinary school, huh?"

"I learned a lot, but I don't like to cook for just myself. That's no fun."

"You must have friends."

"I never see anyone except at the clinic. If I'm not here, I'm studying. I'm desperate for some actual fun. You know, fun?"

"Not really."

"My point exactly. You need to come over and eat a good meal and then—who knows?—maybe I'll let you play with my pussy…cat."

Harper put a hand over her mouth to stifle her laughter, wishing she could see his face.

Seth cleared his throat. But before he had a chance to answer, Mary Lee tapped Harper on the shoulder.

"Patient in three. Not the flu."

It was no use. She couldn't think of a good excuse to linger where she was, so she took the chart and headed for exam three. But, man, she wanted to know.

SHE STARTED THE CAR at six forty-five. Not too bad for a Wednesday. She pulled out of her parking place thinking about what she had to get at the market, when she caught sight of Seth standing by the back door of the clinic. He looked pissed.

She stopped and waved him over.

The way he slammed the door when he got inside let her know that he didn't care for being left behind.

"Sorry," she said.

"What was that about?"

"I, uh, thought you had other plans. My mistake."

"What kind of other plans?"

Her cheeks heated as she tried to come up with an appropriate lie. Unfortunately she sucked at improv, and the few ideas that flitted through her brain were ludicrous. "I thought you might have dinner plans," she said, concentrating on driving and not the waves of anger coming at her.

"Why would you think that?"

She sighed. "I heard Karen ask you, okay?"

"You listened in?"

"I just happened to want a cup of coffee, but before I could get one, I was called to work. So don't be so pissy about it."

"You were eavesdropping."

"A little."

He turned to his window, but she knew he was scowling.

They drove in silence all the way to the market, and Seth stayed in the Ford while she shopped. She was tempted not to buy him any ham or cheese, but she did. And when she got back behind the wheel, she turned to him as she cranked the ignition. "So why are you here?"

"I don't have my own car."

"You know what I mean."

"I do. And it's none of your business."

"But she likes you. I'm not exactly sure why, but she does. And there's no doubt she thinks you're hot. So why not go for it?"

He looked at her as if she'd flashed him. "Are you serious?"

"Of course I am. I mean, really, Seth. Maybe if you got laid…"

"If I *what?*"

"See? It's been way too long. You've already forgotten what it is."

"Jesus, you're amazing," he said, shaking his head.

"I like to think so, but that still doesn't answer the question."

"I'm not going to answer because it's unbelievably insulting of you to ask."

"We're roomies. Roomies get to ask all kinds of things."

"Stop it, Harper."

"Fine. Just let me reiterate. The foul mood thing? It's getting old. And perhaps going home with Karen to play with her pussycat is just what the doctor ordered. If you'll pardon the pun."

"Stop the car."

"We're three blocks from the house."

"I don't care. Just stop the car."

"Don't be silly. We'll be there in one minute and then you can sulk for the rest of the night."

His hand—the real one—slammed down on the dashboard. "Goddammit, Harper, stop the fucking car."

She pulled over, shocked at how angry he was. Okay, so she'd been intrusive, but that was nothing new. What button had she pushed? Was it because of his hand? Did he not feel sexy now that it was gone? Was he kidding?

The second the car was at the curb, he was out the door. As he walked away, she saw his new claw. It looked really cool. Not that she'd tell him that.

HE HAD ABOUT TWENTY bucks in his pocket and no credit card or he would never walk into that house on St. Louis Street. Not ever again. But there wasn't any choice. He was stuck with her. The only way he was getting out of there was to take down Omicron. But how could he do that if he couldn't even mop a floor?

He walked, his left arm heavy and awkward, not looking at the cars or the old houses. He kept thinking about Harper's questions—why hadn't he accepted Karen's invitation?

It wasn't because of his hand. She was a doctor, and it clearly hadn't put her off. It was more than that. Infinitely worse. Because he was cursed—there was only one woman he wanted, and they couldn't get through a drive home without her making him so mad he wanted to strangle her.

He'd tried to think of other women. God knows he'd met some beauties in his life. Incredible women from all parts of the world, and every one of them made more sense than Harper.

He needed to get out of that house. He had to get it together and become a soldier again, even a broken one.

Since he had to be at the clinic anyway, he'd use that as his training ground.

He looked up as he reached her house. He hoped she wasn't in his way, because, dammit, he was ready to fight.

ELI LIEBERMAN SAT IN his apartment, looking at the stack of notes he'd taken from Baker's house. He still couldn't believe that Corky Baker was dead. That this group, this Omicron, had killed him.

He'd never known anyone who'd been murdered. In fact, he'd only been to one funeral in his life, and that was when he was seven.

It was all hard to grasp. Not that he was completely naive about the government. He'd been in the news business long enough to get his feet wet. But this? A rogue arm of the CIA making a chemical weapon to sell on the black market?

Of course, there was a precedent for that. Iran/Contra. And that was the only one the public knew about. For all he knew, this was standard operating procedure. One that would deeply embarrass the government should it be leaked.

He opened one of the notebooks and started reading the barely legible scrawl. He forgot that he'd meant to eat dinner, that he needed a shower. That he had to get back to Vince Yarrow to give him his final decision as to whether he'd continue the investigation or not.

By the time he looked up again, he'd read four full notebooks and come to the realization that there was no decision to make. He was in too deep already just by virtue of finding Baker's body.

Omicron was a monster. A group with money, connections and absolutely no hesitation about keeping their business a secret no matter what.

He was more than likely dead already. The only question left was did he go down fighting or hiding?

Hiding had a lot of good points. He was young, he could disappear without much of a flap. Where? He had no idea. He spoke Spanish, so that was a plus, but...

His gaze hit a notebook, and there on the very edge was a rust-colored stain. The blood of a fellow reporter. Baker had been a bastard, but he'd also been a hell of a journalist. This story would have gotten him a Pulitzer. No question.

One thing for sure—when Eli ran the story, he'd give credit where it was due. He'd make sure that everyone knew exactly how and why Corky Baker had been killed.

He leaned back in his chair, the one his aunt Sophie had given him along with the dining room table and the big, ugly couch. What the hell. Omicron had his name, his address, probably his shoe size. He had no desire to spend the rest of his life in hiding. So it would begin. He would transcribe the notes. He would continue the investigation. And he'd take Vince Yarrow's advice and get himself a big, honkin' gun.

Screw it.

6

SOMETHING WOKE HER. A sound, a bang. It took her a moment to focus on the bedside clock. Two-twelve. After throwing back the covers, she slipped her robe on and went to the hall. She didn't see any lights on and it was very still in the house, and yet she padded down the hall, her bare feet cold on the hardwood floor. When she got to the kitchen, the streetlight outside illuminated the room in a yellow glow, and there was Seth, sitting at the table, a glass in his hand, a bottle of Chivas Regal squat and open nearby.

She thought of retreating, but she'd had enough of this sparring. Whether he liked it or not, they lived together and worked together, and both of their lives would be infinitely better if they could stop sniping at each other.

He jumped a little when she entered the kitchen, but he didn't look at her when she sat down across from him.

"It's late," she said, her voice just above a whisper.

"You should go back to bed."

"Not yet. How drunk are you?"

"Not very."

"You think you could talk to me? Not get angry, just talk?"

He sat for a long time, staring at his glass. Finally he nodded.

"Good," she said. "Hold tight." She had no idea if this was going to be a lengthy conversation, although she hoped it would. Regardless, she needed some fortification of her own. Hers would be tea. Cinnamon-apple sounded right.

It didn't take long for the kettle to boil or for her to spoon out the honey. She took her big mug and sat down again. He'd poured himself another two fingers and he was gripping the glass rather tightly, but at least he was still there.

"What did you want to say?" he asked.

"I'm hoping for a truce."

"We're not at war."

"Aren't we? When's the last time we had a civil conversation? Shared a meal? Laughed?"

Even in the strained light she could see his lips press together. "I'm not feeling very sociable these days."

"I know. And while I grant you that this is a difficult time, we're together a lot. It would be easier if we were friends."

He looked at her now, his whole posture accusatory. "Friends? I think that ship sailed the night you took my hand."

She sighed. "Let's just get through this, okay? I'm a doctor. It's my job to save lives. The way the bullet shattered your hand didn't leave me many options. The nerves were in tatters and the bones destroyed. If I hadn't amputated, you'd never have been able to move even one finger. It was gone, okay? There was no way for me—for any doctor—to have prevented things from going from bad to worse to deadly. I took your hand to save your life. At least this way you have a chance. If I'd listened to you, you'd be dead right now."

"And how do you know that wouldn't have been better?"

"Are you seriously telling me you'd rather have died? Never to know if you could have exposed Omicron for the bastards they are? Never to have the chance to fall in love? Have children?"

He drank again, and when he put the glass down he held on tight. "I don't know."

"Then I did the right thing."

"I'm not…"

"What?"

"I'm not me."

"You are not your left hand, Seth."

"I'm a soldier. A fighter."

"Yes, you are. That hasn't changed."

"You don't know anything about it."

"You don't think we see a lot of vets in the clinic? Men who've lost both legs? Arms gone so high up that they can't fit a prosthesis? It takes time, Seth. Time to heal and adjust. Learn what you can do instead of focusing on what you can't."

"If you couldn't be a doctor anymore…?"

"With one hand, I could be a doctor. I'd have to figure

out ways of doing what I always do, but I'd still have my mind, my training. I wouldn't turn my back on medicine willingly."

He didn't say anything for a long time. Long enough for her to finish half her tea.

"It's not just the hand," he said, his voice different, softer. "It's my folks."

"I know. That must be tough."

"It's their anniversary on Friday. I forget how many years, maybe forty. And they think their only son is a traitor. They think I didn't care enough to call them, to let them know I was alive."

"You'll explain it all to them when this is over. They'll understand."

"I don't understand. How did it all get so messed up? How could our government do this? You know we found a storage facility where they had enough of that gas to kill God knows how many people. Men, women, children."

"But you stopped them."

He shook his head. "We stopped that shipment. We didn't find the manufacturing plant. They could have ten different storage facilities that we haven't found."

"What do you want to be doing now?"

"Not mopping floors."

"I know that. Now answer."

"Working with Nate. I'm the surveillance guy. I'm the one who knows how to hear, to see."

"Does everything you do as the surveillance guy require two hands?"

"Not everything. Just most of it."

"Do you use specialized tools?"

"Not really. I use my hands. It's delicate work."

She nodded. "Maybe while you're mopping floors you could be thinking of ways to modify what you do. There are mechanics who use prosthetics. I know that for sure."

"But not surgeons."

"No, you're right. There may be things you need help with. But first you need to get comfortable with your new claw. Which I like, by the way. Working at the clinic can be the perfect place, if you let it. You're safe there. You have your physical therapy. It can all work in your favor."

He looked at her without speaking. She finished her tea and waited. She could be patient when she had to be.

"What about you?" he asked.

"What about me?"

"What are you doing to stop them?"

"I don't understand."

"You saw what they did. Maybe more than any of us. You were there, in that village."

She nodded. "I wish to God I hadn't, but you're right, I did."

"I know you have the trauma room in case we get hurt, but I also know you aren't happy about it. You don't ask what's going on. You don't ask what you can do to help."

"I'm keeping you here. I got Noah to help."

"All of which is great, but it's not what I'm talking about. You know what I think?"

"What?" she asked, although she didn't really want to know.

"I think you'd be happy if we all just went away and left you alone. I don't think you care a damn that you can't be who you were. I think you like things the way they are."

She got up from the table, but instead of putting her mug in the sink as she'd intended she got out some more tea and put the kettle back on the stove.

"Don't quit on me now," he said.

"I'm not," she said and she heard the testiness in her tone. She'd asked him to talk about some hard stuff, and it was only fair that she be willing to step up to the plate herself.

When she couldn't put it off any longer, after preparing her tea and honey, she sat back down. She looked at Seth. She thought he seemed sad. But then, didn't he always?

"You're right," she said. "I don't relish the idea of fighting with Omicron, despite what I know. I'm not a soldier. I never was."

"Why were you in Kosovo if you didn't want to be in the fight?"

"They told me the war was over."

He leaned back in his chair, but he was still close enough that she could see the expression on his face. She, on the other hand, was in shadow. That made her feel a little better. "I don't have the kind of relationship you have with your family. I wanted to get as far away from mine as I could. Kosovo seemed pretty damned far."

"Why?"

She almost told him it was none of his business, but

she pushed that away. If she ever wanted Seth to trust her, she had to trust him right back. Well, as much as she could. "When I was sixteen, my father went to jail. He was in real estate. We lived in Oregon, in a real nice neighborhood. Our house was one of the biggest in the area, and we had pretty much anything we wanted."

She took a sip of her tea. "One day when I came home from school, there were policemen at the house. A couple of FBI agents were with my dad in his office. They were carting out boxes of his stuff. All his papers and ledgers and just about everything that wasn't nailed to the wall. His real estate business was a scam. He'd bilked hundreds of people out of millions of dollars. Most of them were retired folks with fixed incomes. It hit the papers, was on the news for months. Me and my mom, we lost everything. The house, the car. I had to move in with my grandmother, who would barely talk to me."

"My mother...well, that's another story. But we were never the same again. My father was sentenced to eighteen years and to make restitution. All the money we'd ever had went to that. Including my college fund, even the money for my junior prom dress. I had to go to work after school and all during the summers."

"Shit."

"That's about right."

"So he's still in prison?"

"He gets out in eleven months."

"You going to see him?"

She shook her head. "I haven't spoken to him since he went in."

"What about your mother?"

"Nope. Hey, it's fine. I don't miss it. I've got my work."

"But that's all."

"It's enough."

"That still doesn't tell me why you don't want to fight Omicron. I'd think you, more than most, would want justice."

"You'd be wrong. I just want to be left alone. I hope it all works out, because I think you guys are getting a raw deal. And because I don't want to see any of that gas used ever again."

"But you don't personally want to get involved."

"I'm more involved now than I care to be. Any more questions?"

"Not at the moment. You?"

"Yeah. I still don't get why you didn't go home with Karen."

Seth snorted. "You'll just have to figure that one out for yourself. I'm going to bed."

With that, he stood, took his glass to the sink and the whiskey to the cupboard.

She caught sight of the new claw, and while she could see it looked all high-tech and shiny, she didn't get any details. That could wait till tomorrow.

They'd made progress. She understood a lot more about his frustrations and maybe he understood her point of view. It was a start.

He nodded at her and headed toward the hall.

"Seth?"

"Yeah?" He stopped, turned her way.

"I'm sorry about your parents."

"Me, too."

IT WAS SUNDAY, AND for once, Seth had actually slept late. The morning had been taken up with exercise, followed by an extensive session with the claw. He felt more worn out from that than doing his hundred push-ups.

Finally at four, he'd given it up and taken a long shower, wondering what he was going to do for the rest of the day. Wondering whether Harper was going to stay here or go to the clinic. Hell, he'd been so preoccupied she might have been there and come back.

He couldn't recall when she'd taken time off. Her excuse was paperwork, but he had the feeling it was more than that. The clinic was where she felt safe.

He turned off the water but was instantly on guard as he heard voices. His first reaction was to go for his gun. He didn't have one. He hadn't had one since the night on that lonely highway, trying to save Kate. When the Omicron bastards had shot his hand off. It occurred to him that someone had probably found it. What a gruesome discovery. He hoped it had been a coyote, not a kid.

He dressed quickly, worried about Harper. She hadn't mentioned inviting company, and since he'd been here no one had just dropped by. Even Nate called first.

Not bothering with his hair, his shoes or his claw, he left the bathroom quietly, intending to get a look before he made himself known.

Halfway to the kitchen he relaxed. It wasn't a stranger, it was Nate. And if he wasn't mistaken, that was Kate's voice. His pace quickened, and it was only when he was gripped by Nate's rough hug that he remembered his stump.

He backed away, nodded at Kate and Vince, then excused himself, hoping no one had noticed, knowing they had.

It still took him a while to get everything in place. He wasn't used to the little straps or the way he had to affix the claw. But he finally got the damn thing on, and his slip-on shoes. A swipe with a comb on his too-long hair, and he was ready to face his friends.

What he couldn't do was think of this as anything more than a social call. They were doing fine without him.

"You're looking good, amigo," Nate said when he got back to the party. "Except for that hippie hair."

"Bite me."

Nate laughed. "Now that's the Seth I remember."

Ignoring his old commander, he went to Kate, and she hugged him as if she meant it. He had to admit it felt good. Vince shook his hand, and while Seth didn't know the man well, he'd liked what he'd seen.

"What the hell are you bandits doing here?" he asked.

"We come bearing gifts," Nate said, pointing to the counter by the sink. There were three big brown bags filled, from what Seth could see, with take-out food.

"Barbecue ribs. And brisket. Corn on the cob. Potato salad. Coleslaw. And last but never least, ice-cold beer."

"Holy shit. Where'd you get the dough for this?"

"I just finished a job," Nate said. "I'll fill you in on

that and then we can compare disguises. But first we need to eat."

Harper looked fresh, as if she'd taken the day off to relax. And she was smiling. Any other time he'd seen her with the team, she'd been stressed out and anxious for everyone to leave. He wondered why today was different.

She got out plates and he got the silver. Everyone else pitched in, so the food was on the table in short order. Nate handed out the beer.

It felt good. Like a reunion, like a homecoming. Until he actually sat down to eat. No one had mentioned his claw, which was good, but they obviously hadn't foreseen the problems a one-handed man would face trying to eat ribs.

Not that he couldn't lift the meat and bite down. He could. It was the mess factor. Without the second balancing hand, his control would be terrible and the sauce would get all over his face.

He thought about just eating the other stuff—coleslaw, potato salad. Both could be eaten with a fork and no cutting. The corn? He'd give that a pass. But, dammit, he wanted ribs.

His gaze went from his plate to Harper across the table. She smiled at him and he knew that she got it. There wasn't pity in her eyes, just acknowledgement. That he'd have to figure it out himself. That he'd have to make a choice.

"Hey," he said to her, fighting the urge to whisper. "Do me a favor? Cut these up for me. They look too damn good to miss out on." He pushed his plate to her and she took it with a nod. As she got to work on the half slab, the conversation around him continued as if there'd been no interruption. As if it was no big deal. Which, he supposed, it wasn't. If he didn't let it become one.

Harper pushed the plate back, and now each rib was separate and easy to control. Yeah, he got some sauce on his face, but so did everyone else. "Dr. Hoggly's?" he asked, thinking of the many times he and Nate had gone to eat at the small valley rib joint.

"What else?" Nate said. "Only the best for my team."

Seth grinned, but he couldn't help but wonder if he was still part of the team.

"Did you hear about Baker?" Vince asked him.

"No. I haven't heard much of anything."

"They killed him," Vince said, his nonchalant tone belied by his eyes.

The news slapped Seth in the face. He didn't have to ask who the killers were. When he glanced at Harper, he saw that she knew, too. It was all still out there. Not in the clinic, at least not yet. And not in this home. But that was only temporary. Eventually, inevitably, they would be found.

"He had a lot of information," Nate said. "Another reporter, a kid who works for the *Times,* has taken over. Not sure how effective he'll be, but we don't have a lot of options."

"What kind of information?"

"He was concentrating on Senator Raines. What his connection is with Omicron and where the money is coming from."

"Anything that would stand up in a courtroom?"

"Don't know yet. At the moment, my priority is Tamara. She's getting close. Real close."

"To what?" Harper asked.

"To a dispersal method. The antidote is there and it works, but only when given intravenously. That won't help a village or a schoolyard. She's been working on a way to make the antidote effective if inhaled. And it looks like she might have figured it out."

"Seriously?" Harper looked from Seth back to Nate. "I knew she was smart, but, jeez, that's an amazing accomplishment for one person. Especially in her situation."

"Well, it still needs to be tested," Nate said, and Seth could see he was bothered by Harper's suspicion.

"How's Tam doing?" Seth asked. He knew firsthand how isolated Tam was and how much pressure she was under.

"Okay, considering."

"Are you going to see her anytime soon?" Harper asked.

Nate nodded. "Tomorrow, I think."

"Great." She got up and left the room, presumably to her bedroom. She was gone long enough for Seth to hear the entire story of how they'd found Baker and who the new reporter was.

When she came back, she handed Nate a book. "She lent this to me when we were on the plane from Kosovo. I keep forgetting to return it."

"Sure thing."

Seth watched Harper take her seat again and he knew without a doubt that fetching the book had been nothing but an excuse to get away from the conversation. She hadn't wanted to hear about the reporter's death. Or about Tam. He would bet money that all she wanted was for the discussions about Omicron and the fight to stop and never be brought up again. He wished he could give her that, but she couldn't hide forever.

She looked at him and blushed. He reassured her as best he could with a smile. She nodded once, then she got up to take her dish to the sink.

While the rest of them finished dinner, Nate told Seth about his latest job, a security system for a tech firm in Santa Monica. It felt unreal to hear the familiar terminology again. He'd almost grown accustomed to the medical jargon, but this was his native tongue. He yearned for that world like a child for its mother, and it had never felt so far away.

He didn't reveal a thing. Not during the whole conversation, not when they had coffee, not when Kate told him how she was doing on the Kosovo ledgers. He smiled when he was supposed to and even laughed at the jokes.

The only time he almost lost it was when Harper passed behind him as he sat on the couch with Vince. She brushed his shoulder with her hand, and once again he knew they were on the same wavelength. It was weird having this connection with her. The only time he'd ever experienced anything like it was with his fellow Deltas. It was a matter of survival to know what his team members were thinking. He had a funny feeling that it wasn't so different with Harper.

He had to turn away from his friends and blink away the wet in his eyes. Of all the people…

Later, just before midnight, Nate signaled for him to go outside, to the back of the house. Once they were there in the frigid cold, Nate became all business, as if Seth had never been wounded, as if—

"I thought you might need this," Nate said, holding out a Glock 9mm.

Seth took it in his right hand and used his claw to balance the butt as he looked it over. A box of bullets followed, but Seth took his time with the weapon. It was great, almost identical to the one he'd lost.

"There's a firing range in Covina. Put her away for a minute."

Seth stuck the cold metal behind his back, between his belt and his skin. He shivered, but not from the cold.

"Here's the ID to use. I wouldn't use it anywhere else unless it's urgent. It's not that safe. But I know it'll work at that range."

"I don't know how good I'll be."

"You'll do what you need to. It's hard and getting harder out there, buddy. I need you in top form."

"I won't ever be in top form again."

"Bullshit," Nate said with such assurance that Seth almost believed him. "You'll be different but no less. And one other thing."

"Yeah?"

"Take Harper with you. There's some papers for her in that envelope, as well. When things go bad, they're going to go bad fast. We need everyone up to speed."

Seth wanted to tell him that Harper wasn't interested. But from what Nate was saying, she'd have to get interested, and fast. That would be his job, too. As difficult, he feared, as learning how to be a real goddamn soldier again.

7

TAM WALKED INTO THE lab and turned on the banks of lights. Row after row of fluorescent bulbs flickered to life, making her wish once again that she was somewhere—anywhere—else. Preferably on a sunny beach, with a piña colada in one hand and a hot cabana boy in the other.

She didn't even know if she'd ever see a beach again. Or a movie in a theater. Or a boutique filled with over-priced glamour wear.

She wasn't even thirty yet and she'd probably be dead before her birthday in three months.

A game she played with herself was to try and pick the worst thing about her life. Most of the time it was her parents. She hated that they thought she was dead. Same for her little brother. And her grandma. Yeah, her family won out nine times out of ten. But sometimes it was knowing for sure how much evil there was in the world.

She'd gone into chemistry because she was good at it. Scary good. She'd gotten all kinds of scholarships and awards, a full pass to MIT and a great big paycheck to work for Sheffer Labs. She'd known from the beginning that the contracts were all from the government, and it had bothered her that she didn't know how her work was ultimately used. But the checks, they were so large and she was so young. She was looking at retiring at forty, if not before, with a hefty savings account, a house, a Mercedes convertible and all the time in the world to travel.

She went over to the small table in the corner where she'd set up her coffee supplies. She'd put her foot down when Nate had brought instant. She might have to live like a mole, but she'd be damned if she was going to drink crappy coffee doing it.

It was the money that got her here. Greed, plain and simple. They'd offered her a bundle to do a special project in Kosovo. She'd looked it up on the Internet, read about the war and the UN arbitration. She'd convinced herself that she was doing a good thing, that she hadn't said yes just because of the boatload of money, but there was no denying it now. She'd sold her soul to the devil and he'd taken her straight to hell.

The coffee started dripping, and she put a couple of pieces of bread in the toaster. There was yogurt in the small fridge, strawberry, and she took that out along with the peanut butter. Man, she missed breakfast. She wanted a Belgian waffle. Or a bagel and lox, with red onion and tomato. She wanted a champagne brunch.

But in her little prison it was this or hard-boiled eggs. The bread changed, but it was never really great, and sometimes she had jam on her toast. There was only so much she could cook with a toaster oven, a hot plate and a tiny fridge.

Exercise was another test of ingenuity. Nate had

come through with that, as well. He'd brought her an old treadmill and fixed it up. She ran daily and she did some yoga to a tape. It was probably foolish, considering that it wouldn't matter what she looked like in a casket, but it made her feel more human.

She just wished…

She poured her coffee, added a little skim milk and a packet of sugar substitute. Then she spread her bread with a thin coating of peanut butter. She ate at a small desk, and when she was through, she cleaned, put away, made it look like a lab again.

With her second and last cup of coffee for the day, she thought about what she needed to do next. It wasn't glamorous, but each day she got closer to having the perfect dispersal system. It was taking a very long time, but then, dispersal systems weren't her area. There was nowhere to turn for help. If she didn't do it, it wouldn't get done. People, lots of them, would die. No pressure, right?

She just wished she knew if he was coming by tonight. The visits from Nate saved her sanity. He wanted so much to win this battle, and although he'd never admit it, a lot of his motivation was to get her out of here.

Nate liked her. More than he should. She did everything in her power not to like him back, but he made it difficult.

No matter how optimistic his talk, they both knew the odds of them having a future were not good. Not good at all.

SETH STOOD BY HARPER'S office, wondering if he should close her door. She never left it open when she had a patient. He was pretty sure she'd done it this time by mistake, but he didn't want to interrupt.

The patient was a young black girl who was very pregnant. She was pretty although too thin, especially because she was eating for two. Harper sat in a chair right across from the girl, and while it wasn't possible to hear, he could see that the girl was upset and Harper was trying to calm her.

Instead of walking away, which he should have done, he stood perfectly still and watched. He'd never seen Harper with other patients and her gentleness was something of a shock. She was never like that with him. Her manner was brusque, her attitude flippant. But with the girl, her whole body language was different. Damned if she wasn't holding the girl's hand. Everything about Harper seemed kind and careful. The way she smiled… It was as if he was looking at a stranger.

She was beautiful. All this time he'd thought of her as hot, as tough and gritty, but she wasn't, not right now. The way she smiled was an invitation. Not at all a come-on but something even more intimate. She was asking for the girl's trust in the purest way possible.

Why had she never smiled at him that way? Was it because she didn't believe he would trust her? Shit. He'd never given her any reason to think he even liked her, let alone trusted her.

For the first time since that night, he wished for

something other than to get his hand back. He wished for Harper to smile at him just like that.

The girl was really crying now, and Harper scooted her chair closer. Tissue was used by the handful, but Harper kept touching her. The reassurance of those fingertips was unmistakable. He closed his eyes as his loneliness filled him with regrets so deep his knees almost buckled.

He heard someone close a door, and that was enough to get him moving. Turning around, he went quickly to the janitor's closet and brought out the mop and bucket. He needed to wash the floor in the break room, then the hallway next to the waiting room. He thought about what she'd said to him—that he should be figuring out how to get back to his real work. But before he could focus on that, he had to get a handle on using the claw. Although he was supposed to be able to grip things better, that hadn't been the case. Not yet. He'd spilled his coffee several times, finally giving up and using his right hand to hold the mug. Maybe he'd have better luck with the mop.

The break room was empty, and he filled the bucket with water and the disinfectant soap that smelled like lemon and bleach. He moved the chairs so they wouldn't be in the way and then he gripped the mop handle with the claw. He went at it as if he still had both hands. Mistake. He soaked the bottom of his jeans and his shoes. Rethinking the problem, he realized that he'd tried to use his arm muscles instead of his shoulder.

Take two. This time it worked a little better, only he still made a mess.

"Your rhythm's off."

He spun to find Harper standing at the door. Instantly, as always, his face heated and he wanted to run. Why did he always feel as if she could read his thoughts?

"Try it again, only lead with your left. Let your right hand be your stabilizer."

Instead of telling her to mind her own goddamn business, he thought of her with that girl. It had only been minutes ago that he'd ached for her trust. Considering the talk they'd had, it was up to him, right now, to decide. Did he want to hate her forever? To be alone in that basement with his torment and his pain? Or did he want to accept the fact that while his hand was gone, his life wasn't. It was up to him to make the life he had into something worthwhile. Maybe he couldn't be a warrior. But he could be the man his parents raised him to be. He didn't have to forgive her. All he had to do was keep that information to himself.

He shifted the mop so that his left shoulder was in front. He gripped the handle again, lower this time. Then he tried it again, pushing the mop with the claw, guiding with his real hand.

It wasn't all that bad. Not great, not Army, but he wasn't making a mess either.

"Do you mind if I steal through for some coffee?" Harper said, without an inch of gloat in her voice. "I only have a couple of minutes."

He stopped. "Go ahead."

She stepped around the bucket and the wet and poured herself a cup. When it was to her liking, she headed out again. "Well done," she said. "I'm impressed."

Then she was gone. He continued his work, making sure he didn't miss anything on the floor, but he wasn't even thinking about the mop. He was thinking about Harper. Maybe they could survive the next couple of months. Maybe.

A LITTLE AFTER FIVE, Harper went to the reception area to get some files from Mary Lee. She glanced in the waiting room and stopped cold when she looked at the man sitting by the door. He wasn't a patient. Not only did he look strong and healthy but he wore a business suit, dark, with a plain white shirt and a dark tie. She didn't know a lot about the CIA, but this guy was right out of central casting.

"Did you want something?"

She looked at Mary Lee, who had a file in one hand, the phone cradled at her shoulder.

"Who's that?"

"I don't know. He asked to see you."

"I'll be right back," she said, heading straight for the back of the building, where she'd last seen Seth.

He was in exam room six, cleaning it up for the next patient. There was a discarded paper robe on the exam table next to an old *People* magazine.

Seth turned, and his posture changed the moment he saw her. "What's wrong?"

"There's someone in the waiting room. He doesn't seem right."

Seth headed out into the hallway, pulling his shirt from his jeans. Instead of going toward the waiting room, he went to the back door and outside.

Harper followed, wondering if he was going to ask her to run. She couldn't, of course, unless there was a direct threat to the people in the clinic.

He went to the passenger side of her car and reached beneath the seat. When he stood up again, he had the Glock.

Without even looking at her, he came to the door, shoving the weapon behind his back, into the waistband of his jeans. The shirt fell back down, hiding everything.

"Wait, Seth."

"I can't."

"He could be a patient. Or a salesman."

"If he is, then there'll be no problem."

"It's dangerous to take the gun in there."

"It's even more dangerous to do nothing if that guy is Omicron."

She followed him, practically running to keep up. "How are you going to know?"

"I'll know."

"Seth, stop."

He didn't. He made it to the reception area about five steps ahead of her, and when she reached him, he put his body in between her and the door. She tried to push him aside, but he'd planted himself firmly. She couldn't even see what was going on. "Seth, let me—"

His posture changed again, easing into relaxation. He stepped aside, hugging the door. As she moved into the room, she saw his right hand come out from behind his back.

Without a doubt in her mind, she knew that if the man in the suit had given him a moment's pause, that gun of his would have been primed and ready. Even more unsettling, she knew that he had protected her with more than his weapon—he'd used his body as a shield.

He'd told her more than once that he was a soldier and always would be. She'd be willing to bet for the last few minutes he hadn't given his lost hand a thought. He'd become the warrior. His truest self.

"What's going on?"

Seth nodded toward Mary Lee. The older woman was looking at a catalog of medical equipment. The man in the suit was smiling at her, holding a different catalog. There was no gun, no danger.

"I don't want you in there," Seth said, keeping his voice low. "It may be nothing or it may be reconnaissance. We're not taking any chances."

"He asked to see me."

"Delegate."

She nodded, then stepped back in the hallway. There was a phone a few feet away, and she pressed Mary Lee's number.

"Reception."

"It's Dr. Douglas. Can you take care of the salesman for me? Something's come up."

"Of course."

Harper hung up the phone and turned to Seth. Although he looked exactly the same as he had ten minutes ago, he wasn't the same man at all. Energy came off him in waves, and she wanted to rip off the stupid plastic pieces that changed his face.

"We have to talk," he said as he headed back down the hall.

She followed, curious. Talk about what? The salesman? His job?

He went into her office, and as soon as she crossed the threshold he shut and locked the door.

"Seth, relax, it was just a—"

"I've been relaxed. Too relaxed. I've let this putty on my face lull me into a sense of security. For all we know, that man is Omicron and he's here to make sure you're the doctor from Serbia. He could have heard that I lost my hand and now he's looking for one-armed men. He could be planting a bug right this minute and we wouldn't know."

She opened her mouth, but he wasn't finished.

"That stops now. Tonight. We're coming back here after hours and we're going through this entire place for bugs. Then we're going to put in some cameras so we can keep an eye on things. Tomorrow you and I are going to the shooting range."

"Oh, no. Everything else, fine. I'll help you do a bug sweep and I'll put cameras wherever you say. But a gun? Not for me."

He came close to her, and she had to force herself not to step back. Instead of the broken man trying to master a mop, he seemed huge, larger than life and twice as dangerous. "These people shot off my hand. If they could have, they would have shot off my head. They'll do the same to you. And they won't care who gets in the way. You understand? The people you care for? They'll crush them like ants to get to me. Or you."

"I can't shoot anyone, Seth. It's not in me."

"You know that girl you saw today? That pregnant girl?"

He was talking about Tanesha. Sixteen and pregnant from a rape and she had no idea what to do. "Yes."

"Would you shoot someone to protect her?"

Harper sat down at her desk. Memories of Kosovo flooded her mind, all too vivid. She thought of the babies still in their dead mother's arms. The old man gripping his cane. All the lives the pricks had stolen for money. Because they thought nothing of human lives except their own. "Okay, we'll go shoot. But I warn you, I'm not going to be good at it. I tried to shoot skeet once and I didn't even get close."

"Don't worry about it. You'll learn. I have to call Nate, get some equipment out here. What time does the late shift go home?"

"The offices will be closed after nine."

He got a tiny cell phone from his back pocket and dialed some numbers. Holding it up to his ear, he looked at her once more. "You can go back to work, but keep your eyes open. And I left the mop in exam two."

She hid her grin as she left him, closing the door behind her. "I left the mop in exam two?" she whispered. "Well, my, my."

"NOTHING."

Seth nodded at Nate, then went into the waiting room. It was empty and dark. The empty was good, and the dark didn't matter because they were wearing infrared goggles. It was just the two of them. Like old times. Except it wasn't.

While Seth knew everything to do better than Nate did, in fact, he couldn't do all that much. That pissed him off, but he'd been pissed off plenty of times. Right now he had to make sure that every inch of this clinic was clean.

The moment he'd heard there might be someone who could hurt Harper, he'd…well, he'd gone a little nuts. And it had felt great.

He'd actually felt alive. Fully alive, the way he had back when he was whole. And all he'd wanted to do was save her. Not the patients waiting in the ugly plastic chairs, not Mary Lee, who baked brownies and muffins on Monday mornings. It was all about Harper. The woman he'd been hating for as long as he'd been crippled. The woman he'd been wanting for what seemed like forever.

What did it mean? Probably that he needed to see a shrink. Insanity explained a lot. His letting down his guard. His willingness to be a goddamn janitor. The reason he wasn't sleeping with Harper.

He didn't feel insane now.

"Nothing," Nate said again. He was on the other side of the waiting room, moving slowly, checking for the most sophisticated bugging devices known to man. Seth had his eyes on his own monitor, and so far the room was clean as a whistle.

No one had planted a thing at the clinic. Didn't matter, he was still going to put cameras at the front door, at the back door, at Harper's window, in the reception office. He was still going to teach Harper to defend herself. And he was going to learn to use the claw better than anyone ever had. He was going to be the goddamn world champion one-handed guy.

He would not, under any circumstances, let anything happen to Harper.

8

HARPER SAT IN THE kitchen, sipping tea, wishing she had a friend. She could call Kate or Tam, but they were more associates than girlfriends. Besides, they were the last people she could talk to about this. About Seth.

It was early, barely past five, but she'd been awakened by another nightmare. Exhaustion made her vision blurry and her stomach queasy, but a few more cups of coffee should put her to rights. At least it would get her through the day.

He was still sleeping. She didn't go down in the morning now. He would have to tell her if something was wrong with his stump or his prosthesis. The rest of the healing was up to him.

She missed it, though. Although she hadn't realized it at the time, it had felt good doing something concrete for the team. She'd dreaded the day she'd have to use the trauma room, but when it had come and she'd actually saved Seth's life, a lot of her guilt had disappeared.

She only wished Seth would forgive her. Not so much for her peace of mind as his. Enough time had passed that he should have put things in perspective. It was Omicron who'd landed him here, not her.

Of course, this was exactly why a girlfriend would have been great right now. To talk this thing through. To confirm that she wasn't crazy, but that even while he resented her for taking his hand, Seth was giving her all the signals that he wanted a much more intimate relationship. It sounded nuts, but she couldn't shake the feeling that she was right. Of course, she wasn't all that wise when it came to men and she could be completely off base.

All she knew for sure was that she was lonely as hell. That no matter how much time she spent wearing herself out at the clinic, she continued to have those awful dreams night after night.

The basement door closed, and she glanced at the clock above the sink. Five twenty-eight. What was he doing up?

She heard no footfalls, but when she moved to the hallway, there he was. Damn. He was shirtless, barefoot. The only thing he had on was a pair of blue pin-striped pajama bottoms that rode low on his hips. He didn't even have the sock on his stump, and somehow it made him look far more naked than if he'd ditched the pants.

He was also damp, and it wasn't from a shower. He'd been working out.

"I didn't expect you to be up yet," he said as he crossed the kitchen to the fridge. He took out a bottle of grapefruit juice and uncapped it with his teeth. He spit the cap into the sink, then brought the bottle to his lips.

Harper watched, mesmerized, as he drank. His Adam's apple slid up and down, his neck and jaw muscles tensed and his chest shimmered with sweat. He drank the entire liter, coming up for air only once.

God, he was a stunning creature. Somehow his asymmetry made him even more beautiful. Tragic, mythic. Or maybe it wasn't his wound but his strength in spite of it. All she knew was that her body responded to the man in the most primitive fashion possible. Her breath grew shallow and rapid to match her heartbeat. She squeezed her legs together to ease the sudden pressure. Thankfully she still had some tea to wet her dry mouth.

"Mind if I join you?"

She shook her head. "Be my guest."

"I didn't make any coffee downstairs," he said as he got a mug from the cupboard.

"No problem. You were working out?"

He nodded. "I've got to build up the strength in my left shoulder. I'm doing push-ups."

"You were already doing those."

"Now that my stump is stronger, I'm using my left arm."

"Ouch."

He poured himself a coffee and sat down across from her. "I'm using my pillow, resting it on that. I had to double it to make my body even, but it's working out okay."

"I'm glad. Just be careful. You don't want to go too fast."

He smiled at her. "You've never trained for Delta Force. They do everything too fast, but, damn, it works."

"Okay, have it your own way. I just— Never mind. You know best what you're capable of."

"I don't. Not really. But the only way I'll find out is to take it to the max."

"Well, good. I know you'll feel better if you're in top shape."

He lifted his left arm. "I can work with the claw. I can make adjustments. I'll need to see the attachments that come with the wrist, but I won't need many."

"You do surveillance, right? What does that entail?"

"Electronics. Lots of tiny little bugs that go in places you'd never expect. Long-and short-range listening devices. Computer hacking. All the stuff you see in the spy movies."

"Wow."

"I won't be able to operate like I used to. I'll need someone to be my hands. But I haven't lost any of my expertise. I can still be useful."

She nodded. "What about your weapon? I know you only shoot using one hand."

"It's more than that. I'll have to figure out the best way to reload. And my balance is off. I can't clean the gun the way I used to either."

"It'll certainly keep you busy."

"I have to get this stuff down fast. Now. Nate needs me in the field. I can't keep hiding here."

The thought that he'd be leaving hit her like a slap. She'd bitched about him plenty, but she was finally starting to like him, dammit. "When do you think you'll be going?"

"No idea. I have to figure out where I'll be the most useful. As you pointed out, the last thing they need is to have to babysit me. I've got to pull my own weight."

She almost said something bitchy but stopped herself just in time. This was the most vibrant she'd seen him, and nothing was more effective than spirit for healing. She wasn't about to lead him into an argument.

"What I don't like is you being so vulnerable," he said. "Even with the cameras and the bugs we put in last night, you're a sitting duck. Anyone recognizes you and you're toast."

"Me? I'm not the one on the Wanted posters."

"It's nothing to be flippant about, Harper."

"I know that, Seth, but I can't just lock myself in a closet and hope that things work out for the best. I have to keep busy or I'll go crazy."

He nodded. "Maybe there's something you could do that's less out-there? I've heard you do the street festival, and that can't be wise."

"It's not so much a street festival as it is a quiet little booth three blocks from the clinic where we hand out condoms and AIDS literature. I don't think there are going to be many CIA agents in the market."

"You don't know where they'll be," he said. "That's the point."

"I don't look much like I did in Kosovo. You didn't know me well, but it would surprise me if any of the people I worked with recognized me."

"What's different?"

"My hair, for one. I was a brunette then. And it was much longer. Past my shoulders."

She could see he was trying to visualize her. But he wouldn't succeed. She had also been twenty pounds heavier and she'd worn a lot of makeup. Dark kohl eyes, thinner eyebrows. Frankly she'd looked like a biker chick, which was exactly what she'd been during her residency.

"I like you just like this," he said. His gaze moved slowly over her face, then down to her chest, where the robe crossed over her breasts.

Her hand went to the hollow of her throat as she felt his interest. Saw his eyes dilate. If she said the word, gave him the right look, things between them would change, big-time. But was she ready for that?

How long would he be here, in her home? It could be days, it could be years, there was no way to tell. And while it might be nice to get some while the getting was good, there didn't seem to be a happy ending for any of them.

If it could have been a casual screw, friends with benefits, she'd have gone for it. But it couldn't be—not with what they faced. Intense circumstances came with intense feelings. Their circumstances were quite literally life and death. And she did not do well with intense, not when it came to lovers.

She stood, breaking the connection between them, and poured herself another cup of tea. Even when her back was to him, she felt his gaze, his wanting.

It would be a lie to say she didn't want back. But she could see big red warning lights all over this one.

Seth had almost been killed. Next time, she had the feeling he wouldn't be so lucky. No way she was going to lose her heart along with him. That's not what she'd signed up for. On the other hand, they might kill her first. But, no. Probably not. He was the one they feared. She was just collateral damage.

"I'm gonna go shower. Do you think they could live without me at the clinic today?"

"Of course." She turned to see him standing by the table, his chest a masterwork with six-pack abs. "What are you going to do?"

"Put together the receivers and relays here to see what the cameras are picking up there. Nate and Vince are coming by to help. I'm also gonna get you a gun."

"Make it small."

"I'll do my best."

She nodded, but he was already walking away. Too bad. He looked as if he'd be awfully good in bed.

"She's a good-looking woman," Vince said, watching Harper walk down the hallway at the clinic. They were in the spare bedroom, where Seth had decided to mount the equipment. He didn't have to remove any furniture, just push the bed back against the wall.

When they'd first come in, Vince had smiled so hard Seth had asked Nate about it. Turns out Vince and Kate had stayed in this room right after Seth had been shot.

It wasn't such a good memory for Seth, but he was happy for Vince.

They got to work immediately, all of them settling into a comfortable routine. Nate mostly stood by while Seth told Vince what to do. While Vince was good with a gun, he wasn't that familiar with electronics and Nate needed him to learn as much as he could. The process had been slower than if Seth had done it himself but altogether not bad.

"You and she…?" Vince asked, nodding again at Harper.

"No."

Vince shook his head. "Too bad."

"It's not like that," Seth said sharply. "We still have to put in the wires for the last bank of receivers."

Vince got a roll of coax cable and repeated the process he'd done three times already. Seth watched carefully to make sure he made no mistakes.

"Seems like it would be. Considering."

"Considering what?" Seth wasn't liking this conversation much.

"You know. You're a guy. She's not. Both in the same house. Hell, her bedroom's just down the hall."

"I sleep in the basement."

Vince's eyes widened. "Whoa, what'd you do wrong?"

"Nothing." Seth gave Vince a pointed look, hoping he'd buy a clue and change the damn subject.

"I'd have figured you two would be a natural."

So much for buying a clue. "Could we just get back to business?"

"Sorry," Vince said. "All I'm saying is that it makes it all better, you know? You've been dealt one hell of a crappy hand—if you'll pardon the expression—and being with someone soft and sweet can turn a shit day into something livable."

"Vince, I'm real happy you and Kate got together. But shut the fuck up."

"Got it."

Seth stood. "I'm getting a soda." He didn't wait to hear if either of them wanted one, too.

In the kitchen, he got himself a Coke and drank about half of it before he sat down at the table. What was it with people? He'd liked Vince from the beginning, but the man was treading a very fine line.

Screw it. There were more important things to think about. Like getting her the right gun. He figured a .38 would be just about perfect, and Nate had one at his place. That'd do nicely. He wanted to take her to the range tonight, get them both working on some target practice.

He looked over at where she'd stood this morning. When he'd had to will himself to stay still and not make an ass out of himself.

It was clear she had no interest in him, not that way. He might not have the same body as before, but his instincts about women hadn't changed a bit. She thought of him as a patient. Maybe she was starting to consider him a friend. But that's as far as things went.

He put the soda can on the sink, then headed back to the bedroom. He could only hope that the conversation would stay more focused.

"That's not right," Nate said as soon as Seth entered the room. He was sitting on the bed, looking at the small monitor.

Seth sat next to him and saw exactly what he was talking about. The camera had shifted and was pointing to the floor. "I'm on it."

This was, at last, a task he could complete on his own.

It only took one hand to adjust the camera via the remote wires they'd placed last night. The camera gave a few fits and starts, but eventually it reached a decent angle. Not quite perfect, though.

"There she is again," Vince said.

Harper was in the reception room, looking for something in the file cabinet behind Mary Lee. As they watched, Karen walked into the room and sidled up to Harper.

Nate turned on the microphone. Searing feedback filled the room until Nate got the right meter to obey. A voice replaced the squealing. Karen's voice.

"So where's tall, dark and silent?"

Harper kept on looking for her file. "I assume you mean Seth?"

"I do."

"He had some private matters to attend to today."

"Damn," Karen said. "I wish I'd known."

"You aren't even scheduled to be here until next Tuesday."

"I know. I thought I'd check in for a few extra hours."

"How noble of you."

Karen leaned against the file cabinet, folding her arms over her chest. She wore the same white coat as Harper, but underneath hers was a very low-cut green blouse. "Listen, if I'm stepping into something I shouldn't…"

"What you do with your spare time isn't my concern," Harper said. "But do you think it's wise to pursue a relationship with someone here at the clinic?"

"Wise? Probably not. That hasn't stopped me so far."

Harper turned so her face was clear on the monitor.

She didn't look amused. "Karen, I say this as a friend. Back off."

Karen stood up straight. "Oh, really?"

"Don't."

"Hey, I'm backing off right now. Don't give it another thought."

"Wait a minute. I'm not—"

"Of course not. Perish the thought."

Harper sighed and shook her head.

Seth relaxed. That exchange had been awkward but sensible. Harper knew perfectly well that he couldn't risk getting involved with anyone outside their small group.

Karen patted Harper on the shoulder. "I think I'll go back to Kaiser. See you on Tuesday."

"On Tuesday," Harper repeated, still frowning.

Karen walked out of the reception room, Harper watching her go. The moment she'd cleared the door, Harper smiled. It was wry and small, but it said more than all the words before it.

"No," Vince said. "It's not like that at all."

Nate laughed.

Seth put down the remote and left the bedroom. His blush didn't ease up until he was all the way down in the basement.

9

IT WAS AFTER SEVEN when Nate had finished at Harper's. He was satisfied with the electronics but more so with Seth. It finally felt as if his old friend was back. Given time, Seth would join him in the field. God knows, Nate could use all the help he could get.

Not that Vince wasn't doing an admirable job, but he hadn't been trained the way Nate and Seth had. There was a whole language-barrier thing, too, because Vince hadn't been in the service.

Nate would feel a whole lot better once Seth hit his stride. Things were heating up with Omicron. He and Seth had planted listening devices in the main office in L.A. some time ago, and from what Nate had heard, they were gearing up to make a major sale. So there was another storage facility. The bitch was they still hadn't found the manufacturing plant. There had been a hint, and Nate had sent Boone to Nevada to check it out. Nothing concrete so far.

Vince had told him that their faces were plastered on the walls of every police station in the Greater Los Angeles area. That pressure was coming from high circles to all law enforcement to apprehend without prejudice. And, worse, Cade's cover had been blown. He'd been in Colorado all this time listening in to the Colorado office of Omicron, which, just like their L.A. office, was on its face a military consultancy. They'd found him, traced him to the safe house. Cade was fine, but the house was gone. Burned to the ground. He was on his way here with any data he'd collected, which would be helpful. But, damn. His work in Colorado had been important.

Soon after they'd gotten back to the States, they'd all decided they needed a fail-safe. Somewhere to run if Omicron got too close. Since there was that small branch of Omicron in Colorado, Cade had been chosen to go find a house with a decent basement, then stockpile all the things they'd need to survive. It had to be close enough to Colorado Springs to be able to pick up transmissions from the office there, and he'd found the perfect place.

He'd gotten in, much as Seth and Nate had done with the L.A. office, and he'd planted four microphones. Unlike the Los Angeles branch, it turned out that most of the Omicron business in Colorado was somewhat legitimate. They were consultants who placed soldiers— mercenaries—with armies all over the world.

But Cade had continued to listen in, hoping that he could glean any information that would help the team. It had taken him a full year to get the safe house together. The most important work, other than eavesdropping, had been to dig the evacuation tunnel. The ground was too frozen in winter to dig then, so he'd had to work around that. Finally he'd dug a half mile of tunnel that went from the basement to a hidden valley, where he stowed three ATVs, at the ready. Turns out the tunnel had saved his life.

What had Nate so scared was that Cade's mistake had been so small. He'd made one phone call to his grandfather's house. That's it. He was only on the line for a few moments and he'd never said his name. But Omicron had heard enough.

Not ten days later, Cade had picked up intruders with his motion sensors. He'd taken what he could and made his way through the mountain.

It wasn't all bad. Since Seth wasn't the help he used to be, Nate needed Cade. He was Delta and he understood the stakes. There could be no more errors. Not a phone call, not a misplaced step. It could all come crashing down on them in a heartbeat.

So much depended on what Tam had to say. He'd be at her lab in about forty minutes. She'd called this afternoon, asking him to come by. Something in her voice made him worry, but he didn't want to stay on the phone for even a minute longer than was necessary.

He debated not stopping for supplies, but he couldn't bear to walk into that place without something to cheer her up. That she'd managed to stay sane all this time was a miracle.

Yet another thing to admire her for. She really was the most remarkable woman. Brilliant in a way that almost scared him, she still had a sense of humor in the bleakest of times, still took care of herself when most people would have thrown in the towel. And, Christ, she was…beautiful.

He'd always been lucky with the ladies, but Tam was in a class by herself. A class so high he doubted very much she'd want a thing to do with him once this was over. If it was ever over.

As each day sped past with so little to show for it, his optimism waned. But it was his job to lead. To take point. And he wasn't about to let any of his team down. Not while he could still pull in a breath.

AT SEVEN-FIFTEEN, HARPER walked into the house. She was tired, not so much from work but from the lousy night's sleep. She hated taking sleeping pills, but she'd brought some home. She was forgetting little things, nodding off at her desk. Something had to be done.

As she crossed the kitchen, she slowed and sniffed. If she didn't know better, she'd swear the room smelled like pizza. No, that wasn't right. She headed to the stove, where a half-closed pot simmered. Lifting up the lid, she saw spaghetti sauce bubbling. It smelled wonderful, but what the hell? Seth didn't cook. He made sandwiches.

Had Karen decided to go for him after all? The thought made Harper's throat tight with anger. If they were down in the basement, doing it under Harper's roof—

"Hey, you're home."

She spun around to find Seth, alone, standing in the hall that led to the spare bedroom. "What's going on?"

"We got the clinic wired and I've set up the monitoring system. Well, not just me, but I'll feel much better about you being there. If anyone tries to bug the place, we'll know it immediately and we'll catch it on tape."

"Great, but I meant the sauce."

"Oh." He walked into the room, no prosthetics on his face, his hair all dark and spiky. He had the claw on his left arm, his best, most worn jeans and a white T-shirt that hugged his chest like a second skin. The wires and harness that held on the wrist were visible under his shirt.

She felt like a slug in her old turtleneck sweater and wool slacks.

"I was here and I figured making some dinner would be good practice."

"Dinner?"

"Just spaghetti and sausage."

"It smells great."

He shrugged, but the way he looked at her…something more than dinner was cooking.

"Well, I'm going to jump in the shower."

"Okay. Great." Seth moved a little to the side so she could pass him. He also tried to put his hands in his pockets, then got flustered because the claw wouldn't go.

As she headed to her bedroom, she saw that he blushed all the way down his neck to his chest, in addition to the traditional cheek thing.

He was flustered. She had the feeling it wasn't just because he'd forgotten about his hand but because she'd witnessed it.

Damned if she didn't feel his gaze on her all the way

down the hall. When she turned to shut her door, he glanced away too quickly.

What was she going to do about him?

TAM SMILED THE MOMENT Nate entered the lab. He smiled back, holding out his offering. A big salad, the kind she liked, with some grilled fish and crusty bread. For dessert, he'd brought a couple of slices of key lime pie.

Her eyes lit up as she opened the containers, especially when she got to the pie. "I haven't had key lime in so long. How did you even know it was one of my favorites?"

He shrugged, not wanting to admit that she'd mentioned the fact one night about seven months ago, when he'd brought tuna sandwiches.

"You got enough for two. That means you can stay for a while?"

He nodded. "Let's eat and then you can tell me what all the mystery's about."

She got out a couple of real forks, two bottles of water and paper towels, then led him into her bedroom. It was the only place she could escape from work. Everything that was personal, that was Tamara, was in this tiny room. It only allowed for a twin bed, a small used dresser and a box where she put her TV.

At least he'd gotten her cable. What the hell, he was already wanted for treason, he might as well add cable theft to the charges. Besides, no one deserved the R & R more than Tam.

They'd at least tried to make it livable here. There had

already been a shower in the room directly behind the bedroom. Seth had fixed it so she got hot water, which she'd been very grateful for.

She made a fuss over the grilled fish and tried to give him the big piece. He refused and she didn't argue. That told him a lot.

For the next half hour they ate, drank their water, enjoyed sitting on the bed together, plastic containers teetering on their laps. When it came to the pie, Tam moaned in a way that made him uncomfortable, not that he let on.

He had time enough to wish that he had brought wine, maybe a few new CDs for her small system. She was too pale. It was ridiculous that she should be trapped here.

Maybe he should get her some new clothes. Harper or Kate would know her size. He wanted to see her without that damn lab coat. In something other than jeans. Although, he had to admit, she did her jeans proud.

It was something of a relief when the trash was tossed and they were back in the lab, where both of them were on more stable footing.

She went to her favorite perch, a stainless-steel countertop that was just a bit lower than the others. She hopped up, pushed her hair back and gave him a sly smile.

"What's going on, Tam?"

"Oh, nothing much," she said. "Just that I'm pretty sure I've done it."

"Seriously?"

She nodded. "I really think I've worked out the last of the problems. But I won't know for sure until I can test it."

"So what are you waiting for?"

"To paraphrase a famous line, we're gonna need a bigger lab."

"How much bigger?"

"Well, I think I could make do with the chemistry facilities at UCLA, but I'm not certain."

He ran a hand over his face, suddenly so tired that it was an effort to keep his head up. He didn't have any money left. There was a job coming up, but that wouldn't happen until next month. He had no idea how to break into the chemistry facilities at UCLA. His people were hurting and tired, his options were few and time was running out. What the hell was he supposed to do?

"Nate, are you okay?"

"I'm fine. Let me think about this, okay? I'll come up with something."

She reached into her coat pocket and pulled out a single sheet of paper. "I printed out a priority list. Things I have to have, things I can jury-rig, things that would be nice but are not vital."

He took it, but he barely gave it a glance. Tomorrow he'd feel better. He'd talk to Harper. Maybe she knew someone at a chemistry lab or drug company. He'd take any suggestions about now, as he was tapped out.

"You don't look so great," Tam said, sliding off the counter. She touched his forehead with the back of her hand. "No temperature. Are you sure you're okay?"

"I'll live," he said, then instantly regretted the admission. He couldn't be down around Tam. She needed all the positive energy she could get. "Actually, today was good all the way around. Seth's really coming along."

"I'm glad. From what I knew of him, he seemed like a great guy."

"He is. And a hell of a soldier. It'll be good to have him back."

"I have a somewhat radical idea," she said.

"Oh?"

"How about you get away for a couple of days? Go somewhere nice, like Palm Springs. Get drunk. Go sit in a hot tub. And don't think about Omicron or chemical weapons for even a second."

He shook his head. "Me? I'm not stuck in this pit day after day. It's you who should get out."

"If things go well, my part of this will be done very shortly. Once we have an antidote that can be delivered, I'm out of here. But that just starts a whole new set of problems for you."

"We'll get through it. The object isn't just to have an antidote. It's to get rid of the weapon altogether. To expose the pricks behind it and take them all down."

"Which probably isn't going to happen tomorrow. Which means that you could get away for a couple of days without the world coming to an end."

"Come with me."

"What?"

"You need the rest as much as I do."

She blushed, her cheeks turning a really nice pink. When she looked at him again, there was a shyness there he'd never seen before.

He wanted to take it back. Not that going away with Tam would be anything but great, but he didn't want it to be like this. He most especially didn't want to scare her. "Separate rooms, of course," he said, hoping he didn't sound as desperate as he felt.

"I thank you for the invitation, but I still have a lot to do. I want the antidote to be a viable threat to Omicron's business. It can't be that unless I can deliver it to a large area very quickly."

"Granted. But you know, I was thinking…what about crop dusters? Do you think those could work?"

"Maybe. It's a good idea. But the spray mechanism isn't as important as the viability of the antidote through atmosphere and it's stability. People have to breathe it in for it to work. It can't deteriorate in rain or humidity or bright sunlight. There are a hundred questions I won't be able to answer, not even if I had years to work on it, but the basic things must be true for this to be a weapon against that horrible death."

"Okay, I'll work on the lab. I promise. We'll find what you need."

Her hand, the one that had touched his forehead, went to his arm, where she squeezed him gently. "I know. You'll come through. That's who you are. Only, don't let the stress cripple you, okay? Remember that, despite the evidence, you're only human."

Another place, another time, he would have pulled her to him and kissed her until she couldn't remember how to speak. "I'd better be going. Lots to do tomorrow."

"Thanks for the meal. And the dessert."

He smiled, nodded, headed out the door and up into the crapped-out building that hid her. Once he was finally at his car, he didn't start it right away. He put his head down on the steering wheel and closed his eyes. He wanted her. He wanted Omicron to burn in hell. He wanted so much, and his chances of getting any of it were between slim and none. Some nights, those odds were just fine. Tonight wasn't one of them.

SETH SERVED HER. HE had to ladle the pasta onto the plate, put the ladle down, pick up the plate and take it to her, but he got it done with only minor spattering. It was just weird to have to think about something as simple as dishing out spaghetti. In the old days—

He stopped himself short. He'd never get anywhere if he constantly thought about what had been or what should be. His best chance of success was to be in the moment. Take the next step. Do the next logical thing.

"This looks wonderful," Harper said, smiling at him as if he'd just painted the Sistine Chapel.

"It's spaghetti."

"That's right. But it's pasta, not ham and cheese. This is major."

He gave her a scowl, then went back and served himself. He'd already poured them each a half glass of Chianti and put the garlic bread—store-bought, but heated by him—on the table. Too late, he realized that she probably would have wanted a salad. She hadn't said anything, but still, she would have liked that.

He finally had his plate full and went back to sit

down. She'd sipped some wine, but she hadn't tasted the food. "Is something wrong?"

"No, why?"

"You haven't eaten."

"I was waiting for you."

"Why?"

"Because I wasn't raised by wolves."

"Oh. Well. Thanks."

"You're welcome."

She twirled some pasta on her fork, and halfway through chewing she made a really great sound.

He took a bite himself. Not half-bad.

"Seth, it's terrific."

"My mother used to make this a lot. I think I got pretty close."

"Close or not, it's wonderful."

He ate to cover his grin and hoped she didn't see how much her praise meant. He'd wanted this night to go well, not just because it was good practice but because… Shit. He was getting ahead of himself and he shouldn't do that. Just because she'd smiled. It could have meant anything. Seth had no real knowledge of Harper's relationship to Karen. So it probably didn't have a thing to do with Harper feeling proprietary about him. Or wanting there to be more than friendship. He couldn't afford to assume a damn thing.

Only, it was hard to deny that she'd smiled an awful lot since she'd come home. Or that she'd touched his arm five times.

But there were miles between dinner and bed.

They ate in companionable silence. She finished everything on her plate, and he decided against seconds. It was almost nine when there was no more food to distract them.

Seth had no clue what to do. Did he say something? Touch her? Just lean over and kiss her? Mention that instead of taking her to the firing range, which he should have done, he wanted to take her to bed?

"I'm stuffed," she said. "If you leave the dishes in the sink, I'll get them in the morning. I'm just too tired to do them tonight."

"No sweat. I've got it," he said, cursing his own stupidity. Thank God he'd kept his thoughts to himself.

Harper stood, kissed him on the forehead, then headed to her bedroom without so much as a backward glance.

It took him a long time to gather the will to stand, let alone clear the table. But he did, one stinking dish at a time.

10

THERE WERE NO FLIES around the bodies. The air was still and calm, so there should have been swarms of flies at this deathly feast, but they were smarter than the humans who kept searching for someone, anyone, alive.

It was VX gas, it had to be. Nothing else was more deadly. They had all been killed so quickly. Their rigor showed their horror and outrage, clutching each other while everyone they knew fell into spasms, as foam bubbled from their mouths, as their eyes filled with blood.

Who had done this? Why? This was a small village of poor people, scrounging through their days to put bread or a chicken on the table. These were children. Babies.

She didn't know, didn't care, about the war. She wasn't here to do politics. All she'd wanted was to treat people who had little or no access to health care. To teach the women how to save their children. To teach them all how to not get AIDS.

Nothing, not even the battle zones, had prepared her for this. She kept choking up, unable to see through her tears, but she didn't want to wipe her eyes. She knew if it was the kind of chemical agent she suspected, it was inert by now. But she'd touched so many of their bodies. The lack of flies told her something was wrong, some signature of the gas lingered. And if she touched any part of her mucous membrane, she could be next.

She stepped over a young woman with long braids, and her foot landed on something small and soft. She looked down to find a bird. A pigeon. Next to the bird was a boy clutching a toy truck. His red eyes were open, staring right at her.

She gasped. And then she was in her room, in her bed. Disoriented, she struggled to the side of the bed, reached for the lamp switch. And then she looked toward the door. It was open. She never left it open.

"Harper?"

The low male voice belonged to Seth, not the men who'd killed the village. The relief hit her so intensely that the tears she'd held back in her dream came out with a sob.

The side of her bed dipped and his hand was on her shoulder. "What happened? What's wrong?"

She shook her head, unable to speak. She hadn't cried in so long, not even when the nightmares tore her apart. It hurt her throat, she sobbed so hard.

Seth pulled her closer, and she leaned against his chest as she abandoned herself to her weeping. She didn't care anymore. What she'd seen had mutilated her as badly as the bullet had maimed Seth. She simply couldn't hold it in any longer.

His hand rubbed her shoulder, his breath brushed her neck. He whispered soft words, trying to calm her, but nothing could. At least she wasn't alone. He was here, he was warm. Strong. He was a warrior and she was safe with him. At least for tonight.

She'd never been one to pray, but she found herself pleading to not die like that. A bullet would be better. Anything would be. She just didn't want to die like those people.

"Shh," he whispered again.

Her sobs had turned to intermittent hiccups and her tears didn't burn quite so much. She wished she had a tissue, though, because she was soaking his chest. His naked chest.

Her hand went down to his thigh, and, yes, he was in his pajamas. Had she awakened him all the way down in the basement? "I'm sorry," she said between sniffs.

"For what?"

"Waking you."

"You didn't. I couldn't sleep. I heard you cry out."

She used the back of her hands to wipe some of the moisture from her face. "It's okay. You can go back to bed. I'm fine."

"You call this fine?"

"It was just a nightmare."

"Harper, you sounded like you were going to die."

She sat up, grateful as hell she hadn't turned on the light. "I was. In my dream."

"You want to talk about it?"

She shook her head. "No. I want to forget about it."

"What can I do?"

She smiled. He was so big and tough, yet his voice

sounded like a boy's. "Nothing. Really. I'm good. I'll just get some tea, then go back to—"

"You won't do anything. I'll bring you the tea."

She sniffed again, unbelievably happy he was there. "Have you ever in your life made tea?"

He nodded. "Yeah, I have. You like yours with a little honey, right?"

"I do."

"Okay. You wait right here. I'll be back in a flash." His hand left her shoulder and his arm abandoned her back. She was alone again, only not quite as alone as before.

Was he the answer to her nightmares? Normally it took her hours to come down from the shaky terror, but not tonight. And tonight had been the worst she'd ever had. Maybe they'd go away completely if he slept up here. In here. In her bed, so she could feel his solid chest and his soft breath on her neck.

She shifted in the dark, her thoughts dipping into a whole different kind of rescue.

If she asked him to stay for the night, it would be perfectly understandable. And if they touched, well, it wasn't that big a bed.

She had no desire for tea. Just for Seth to come back.

He wanted exactly the same thing, but he had to do this right. He boiled the water, let it cool for one minute, poured it into her big mug along with her favorite apple-spice, then waited, the seconds ticking slowly inside his head, until it had steeped for four minutes. It could have gone five, but screw it. He got the honey and gave her one teaspoon of the stuff, stirred it, then headed tentatively back to the bedroom.

He breathed a huge sigh of relief when he saw it was still dark in there. If she'd turned on the light, he'd have been in big trouble. Damn flimsy pajama pants.

It occurred to him that he wasn't the least bit worried about disguising his stump, but he'd very much like to have a heavy pair of Levi's to hide his hard-on.

He slowed even more as he got to her door. If she was sleeping, he'd back out.

"It's okay," she said. "I'm awake."

"I wish you weren't," he said, lying through his teeth. "But maybe this'll help."

He got to the bed without a mishap. The closer he got to Harper, the clearer she became. He wasn't certain it was all because of his eyes adjusting to the dark. He'd pictured her just like this, waiting for him, so many nights, so many early mornings, that he could paint in all the details. He wished she hadn't had the nightmare, though. And that she'd given him any reason to think she might like him to stay.

She took the tea, sipped it. "Perfect," she said. "How would you feel about spending the night here?"

He couldn't have heard that right. "Pardon me?"

She patted the bed next to her. "Sleep with me. Please."

If he hadn't had a hard-on before, he would've gotten one just from hearing those words. As it was, his condition did grow more serious. But she'd said *sleep,* and that's probably all she'd meant. So he shouldn't get too excited.

Wait. Too late.

"Uh, Seth?"

"Yeah." Shit. His voice had broken. He cleared his throat and tried again. "Yeah."

"If you don't want to, that's all right."

"No, no. No. No."

She did a little throat clearing of her own. "I'm making you nervous."

"No. Well, yes. But it's okay."

"Get into bed. That'll make things a little easier."

He nodded, then went around to the other side of the bed and slipped under the covers. It did make things easier. At least his dick wasn't sticking out like a tent pole.

"This tea really is perfect. Just the way I like it."

"My mother likes her tea like that."

Harper's hand touched his side. "Tell you what, let's not talk about mothers right now, okay?"

"Sure. Okay."

She laughed so quietly he felt as if he was eavesdropping. "I appreciate you doing this for me," she said, her voice still low. "I've been having these wretched nightmares for months. They're all pretty much the same."

"Kosovo?"

"Serbia, actually. The day I went into the village."

She didn't have to tell him which village. There was only the one that really mattered to them. The one that someone in Omicron had decided had the most expendable citizens. The one they'd used as the testing ground for their death gas. "I'd forgotten," he said, "that you were there first."

"I wasn't alone. But, yes. I was the first to see."

"Jesus," he said, barely able to imagine the horror, even after all he'd seen and done.

"Yeah."

"You've been dreaming about that every night? How can you even face going to bed?"

"It's not easy. Why do you think I work so hard at the clinic? I try to exhaust myself."

"But it doesn't work."

"It gets me to sleep. It just doesn't keep me asleep."

"Have you thought about seeing someone?"

She laughed. "Now how come it's so easy for you to ask me that, and when I try to ask you the same thing—"

"Yeah, yeah, I'm a stubborn ass. You're the one with the brains."

"I don't know what a doctor would do. Of course I've read everything I can about night terrors, but I'm not sure what's happening to me fits. I think there may actually be a couple of solutions."

"What?"

"We take down Omicron and make sure that gas is destroyed completely, along with how to make it."

"Or?"

"This."

"What?"

"You. Here. With me."

"Oh."

She put her tea down on the bed stand, then turned to face him. He wished he could see more, especially her eyes. But he didn't want the lights on. Not yet.

"I think I should make myself clear. I'm not asking

you to be my boyfriend or anything. But, hell, who else am I going to turn to? It's been pretty crappy for the both of us. So why not take some comfort where we can?"

He thought for a long moment, trying to phrase this right. "So when you say *comfort*…"

There was that tiny laugh again. Only this time, it was followed by a not-so-tiny kiss.

Harper leaned into him, then parted her lips. She didn't know if it was the lateness of the hour or the after-effects of the dream, but she wasn't in the least interested in beating around the bush.

She'd known Seth for a long time now, and aside from the fact that he still hadn't forgiven her for saving his life, he was, down deep, a really good man. She didn't have to lie to him about a damn thing. She didn't have to promise him anything either. They were both on the edge of disaster every single day, and frankly she'd rather not go out alone.

Not to mention he was, when not being a horse's ass, hot as hell.

He hadn't done much since she'd gotten him into bed, and frankly she was getting a little concerned. And then—boom—he rose to the occasion.

He brought his hand to her neck and held her steady, not forcing, not hurting, but she knew he meant business. What had a second ago been cool, vaguely pliant lips became a mouth on a mission.

He plunged his tongue into her as if she were the last safe place on earth, and his moan was that of a man who'd found heaven.

She'd never been kissed like this before, as if she was a goddess or a movie star. She'd known passion and she'd known that red-hot heat of having to do it right that minute or die, and yet this was that squared.

How long had it been since he'd gotten laid? Not that she was going to interrupt to ask. But, damn, it must have been aeons, because holy crap.

His lips left hers for a moment to explore her neck, which should have given her a chance to catch her breath, but the effect was the opposite. He electrified her, stole every bit of the air from the room, and when he nipped, then licked the sensitive skin under her ear, she shivered all the way to her toes.

She wrapped her arms around his back, mostly so she could feel more of him. He had such an incredible body. Bless the U.S. Army for its training. She must remember to send a fan letter to the guy in charge.

His hand left her neck to glide down her back. She was still in her sleep shirt, but not for long. She let him go, pulled back and tore the stupid thing off.

Seth, a quick learner, maneuvered his pajama bottoms off and tossed them to the floor. He pulled her back, but she put a hand on his chest. "Wait."

"Why?"

"Condoms."

"What about them?"

"I have some in the bathroom."

"I don't care."

"You also don't get pregnant."

That stopped him. "Oh, right. Where in the bathroom?"

"You stay here. It'll be faster if I go."

He nodded. In the faint light that came through her window she could see his pout. It was as sweet as it was silly, as she'd be right back. But, just to give him something to do, she threw back the covers.

There he was, all buff and naked, and she thought about turning on the light so she could see him better. But then he could see her better, so no. But what she did see was pretty amazing.

To say he had an erection didn't give him nearly enough credit. He might not have been the biggest guy she'd ever seen, but he certainly was the most enthusiastic.

She took his hand, put it on his cock and said, "Amuse yourself. I'll be back in a sec."

Before he had a chance to react, she was out of the bed and hurrying to the bathroom. Unfortunately she had to turn on the light in there, as it was pitch-black. She closed her eyes, flipped the switch and waited until her eyes had adjusted.

The moment she could, she ransacked the drawer next to the sink where she knew she'd put some condoms. She tried to remember when that had been, but it didn't matter. They were going to be used tonight.

There. She found not one but two little gold packets. Hallelujah.

Instead of turning off the bathroom light, she left it on. It didn't make the bedroom too bright but just right.

The first thing she saw, in fact, was that Seth had obeyed orders. He was stroking himself, and she had to admire his technique. Long and slow, from the base to the tip.

He'd leaned back against her headboard and he was watching her through heavy-lidded eyes. She let her own gaze linger on his handsome face, his strong jaw, that amazing chest, all the way down to his cock. He was perfect in every detail—and, no, she wasn't forgetting a thing. He truly was gorgeous.

She forced herself to walk slowly, to let him look at her the way she'd looked at him. It wasn't that she was ashamed of her body so much as she wasn't used to being so open. So vulnerable.

What kept her going was the expression on his face. Much like his kiss, his eyes told her that he was more than pleased. That she was extraordinary, to him at least. It was a heady feeling and damn good for the libido. A thought crossed her mind, but it was stupid, unreal. What she saw on him was lust, pure and simple. Nothing more. Hell, she didn't want more. She'd tried to imagine being in love, being loved back, but she'd never gotten past the absurdity of the concept. His lust? That she could handle.

She crawled back onto the bed on all fours, feeling sexier than she could ever recall. His hand stilled and then he reached for her. She kissed him and he kissed her back for a long time. And when she couldn't stand it another minute, she straddled his thighs and rubbed her breasts against his chest.

"Oh, yes," he whispered as his head went back against the headboard. "Harper."

"You think that's fun," she said, "just wait."

He moaned, and she bit the tip of his jaw, then used her teeth to open the condom wrapper.

She could feel him, pushing insistently against her butt, the little round head all wet and eager. Of course, she had to lift herself pretty high to get in the right position, but then he stepped in and held his cock still while she rolled the latex down.

The moment it was done, he shifted his hand to her waist. She moved again, this time getting herself lined up.

She could feel him trembling with the effort not to push up with his hips, to wait until she made the move.

He didn't have to wait long.

11

HE COULDN'T BELIEVE it was happening, that she was so beautiful and so willing. He wouldn't push up, he wouldn't, not even if he died from the anticipation. Finally, though... "Please."

She smiled at him, a long, slow grin that made his chest constrict. As she lowered her body, he struggled between squeezing his eyes shut to drown in her wet heat or watching her face. He couldn't close his eyes. Not when there was so much to see.

Her head had gone back, revealing the arch of her neck. He wanted to kiss her there again, but he couldn't move. At least not much. So he did what he could—he touched the tip of her nipple with his fingers, then spread his hand to cup her perfect, small breast.

She leaned into his hand as she worked her thighs, raising and lowering herself in a maddeningly slow rhythm.

It was so good, so much better than his pitiful imagination.

"Seth," she said.

"Hmm?"

"You're grinning."

"I'm happy."

"I bet you are."

"What's that supposed to mean?"

She closed her eyes for a moment as she settled on him, moving her hips in a wicked circle. "I've seen you, you know."

His hand gripped her breast and she gasped. He let go instantly.

"No, it's okay," she said, putting his hand back.

"What do you mean you've seen me?"

"I have. Hungry little stares when you thought I wasn't watching."

He snorted. "Conceited much?"

She laughed and then she squeezed him back, only it wasn't with her hand.

His head banged against the headboard, but he didn't feel a thing. "I don't think I can do this much longer."

"You want me to stop?"

"No. Yes. No. I mean, I can't stay so still."

"Who said you had to?"

Before the words had settled, he gripped her waist with his right hand, balanced her side with his stump, then used his hips to flip her onto her back.

She cried out, but from the rapid rise and fall of those excellent breasts and the smile on her face, he didn't think she was hurt.

The problem was that he was no longer inside her. It only took a moment to spread her legs with his knees, but he was off balance. It was the damn stump. She followed his gaze, pulled a pillow from the far side of the bed and folded it in half. Then she put it on her right side next to her shoulder. Exactly where it would work the best.

"You are amazing," he said.

"I know."

"And modest."

She laughed as she ran her hand down his chest.

He settled himself over her, grateful he'd been doing his push-ups. The stump didn't hurt at all and—oh, yeah—he had his balance now. What he didn't have was a free hand to guide his cock, but the astonishing Harper took care of that, too.

Once he was in, he took point. Her smile disappeared as he gave in to the overwhelming need to go deep. Go hard. He thrust into her, shaking the whole bed, but it wasn't enough. He pulled back and slammed home, and she cried out, her fingers scratching at his back, her legs curling up around his ass, urging him for more.

He did it again and again, until sweat blinded him, until his arms trembled, and she kept rising to meet each thrust. He grunted, swore. And then it was there, the tightness in his balls, in his gut, and he lost any control he might have had as he came.

Harper opened her eyes as the climax took him. His face twisted up with the strain and release, but all she could see was the warrior. He bared his teeth and groaned like a wild man, and it was so erotic, so primal, she came again herself. Or maybe it was just a continuation of the one that had hit after two minutes of him on top.

He collapsed, thoughtfully, to her left. She closed her

eyes and tried to get her breathing under control. They sounded as if they'd just finished running a marathon, which they kinda had.

Selfishly she was glad he'd worn the condom so that she didn't have to get out of bed to clean up. All she wanted to do now was sleep. God, she hoped he didn't want to cuddle.

"Shit," he said.

"I know."

"You okay?"

"Fabulous. You?"

"Worn out."

"Me, too," she said. "So you won't take offense if I get some sleep, right?"

He turned his head to look at her, and she could tell she'd shocked him. "You want me to go?"

"No. You can stay if you want to. But I'm sure I won't have another nightmare tonight."

He didn't say anything for a while, probably deciding how to feel about things. Hell, she'd told him up front what she wanted. He should be pleased. No pretense, no faking it. They'd both needed a good fuck, and now that they'd had it, they could move along.

She sat up, pulled the covers from the bottom of the bed, then turned on her side to go to sleep. A moment later he rose and headed for the bathroom. She was asleep before he returned.

SETH GOT UP AT FIVE, although he'd been awake a while. Mostly he'd just watched Harper sleep. She was very quiet, very still, and he was glad that she was able to get the rest she needed. But what the hell?

Not that he'd expected a declaration of undying love, but jeez. Slam, bam, thank you… He guessed there wasn't a little rhyme for the women who wanted it fast, hard and unemotional.

The truth was, he didn't understand why he was so uncomfortable. He'd never been the kind of guy to turn over and go to sleep, so maybe it was just the surprise of it. She had never said she wanted anything but sex, and God knows that's all he wanted, so what was the problem?

Something else had to be going on, that's all. Some psychological thing about his hand maybe.

He went down to the basement and started his workout. Old habits kicked in, and he thought of nothing but the muscles, the count, breathing right, keeping the perfect position for each exercise. When he finally finished, he thought about going back to bed—his bed—but it was after six and he didn't want to waste the day. He gathered his clothes and went upstairs to the guest bathroom.

The second he was in the shower, thoughts of Harper and the way she'd left things filled his head. Not being a shrink, he had no idea what kind of weird psychoses came along with losing a limb, but one of them was probably the need for extra reassurance when it came to the bedroom. She'd actually given him the best reassurance of all—it hadn't mattered. She'd been quick to provide assistance when he'd needed it, but that was it. No drama, no trauma. Which was exactly what he'd wanted.

And yet her turning over like that… He'd been, well, hurt. The thought made him wince. He was Delta Force, hand or no hand. He knew exactly where sex fit into the program and where it didn't.

He wasn't looking for a relationship or a lover or anything close to it. His priorities were clear—train until the hand was a nonissue. Take down Omicron. Don't get dead. It didn't get more uncomplicated than that. And wasn't it convenient that he and Harper could get their rocks off together. No need to worry about bringing some civilian into this.

The whole situation was a dream come true. So what was his deal?

He soaped up, washed his hair, told himself to stop being such a pussy. He had decided to go to the clinic. It was still his responsibility, at least until they hired someone to take his place. Only, he was going to cut his hours. This afternoon he was going to connect with Nate. They needed to figure something out to help Tam run her tests. Then tonight he'd finally take Harper to the shooting range.

It wouldn't do any good to keep analyzing the situation with Harper, so he wouldn't. Not even to wonder if he should sleep with her tonight.

ELI LIEBERMAN SAT IN his Toyota—the one he'd had since he was nineteen, and he'd bought it used. While he was grateful for the reliability, it was far from his dream car. That was a Porsche 911 Turbo, and he'd been dreaming about that baby for years.

If he went to the editor of the *Times* with the information he had in the trunk, odds were high that he'd never get his Ferrari. He'd never get married, have kids, go to Bali. Because he'd be dead. Dead like Corky Baker. Dead like all those people in Serbia.

It was crunch time. Take over the story or let Omicron and the CIA and Senator Raines get away with murder.

He would have liked to think that there would be no question, that he'd do the right thing because he was an honorable man. But it wasn't that simple.

Ever since he'd discovered Baker's body he'd been terrified out of his mind. He was pretty goddamned sure he was being followed. He'd stopped using his phone at the apartment, bought a gun and was at the shooting range every single night. And he'd pretty much stopped sleeping.

He'd transcribed it all, seen the implications, and it was not pretty. He wasn't even sure he could convince the editor that it was the truth.

The scary part was, he believed every word.

He thought about his folks. Briefly he'd considered asking their advice. But he didn't want them to know how real the danger was. On this one, he was flying solo.

So what was it to be? Forget he knew anything about this and go on with the rest of his life? Or risk it all to expose the truth?

HARPER FINISHED WITH her ninth patient of the day, and instead of wanting to drink an entire pot of coffee, she actually felt ready to do more. She couldn't believe how well she'd slept. And how amazing it had been with Seth.

She hadn't seen him much today, although she knew he was out there working. But when she had, he'd seemed distant. Quiet. More like when he'd first come to work here.

Having never claimed to understand the male mind, she headed out to the waiting room to let Mary Lee know she wasn't going to take a break. Since they closed early tonight, she wanted to finish with the last of the patients. There was another doctor and a nurse-practitioner here, so between them they should be out of here soon. She'd promised Seth nothing would stop them from going to the firing range tonight, even though she dreaded it.

Speak of the devil, there was Seth by the big cabinet, stuffing files back in alphabetical order. He'd gotten pretty good at using the claw. He improvised now as a person would do once they'd accepted the facts of the matter. It hadn't occurred to her until this morning that his hand might have been an issue during sex. And that was because it hadn't been.

It all went back to that salesman. That had been the moment Seth had left his victim mentality behind.

"Mary Lee?"

The older woman put out her hand for a moment as she finished some notes on a file. Harper glanced at Seth, who turned his head as soon as she met his gaze.

"What did you need, Dr. Douglas?"

She sat down in the guest chair next to Mary Lee. "First, did Seth tell you he'll be leaving us?"

"Oh, no." Mary Lee looked over at Seth. "I'll be sad to see you go."

Seth cleared his throat. "Thanks."

"When will that be?"

"When you hire my replacement."

The older woman smiled. "That's very nice. I'll put an ad in the paper in the morning."

He nodded, then turned back to his filing.

"Was that it, Dr. Douglas?"

"Just wondering who we have out there."

"Well," Mary Lee said, "we've got Ms. Landry, who's here for some birth control. Dr. Cavell is already with Mr. Taylor. That leaves Mr. Smith, who wanted to have a consult with you about some stomach ailment." She leaned closer to Harper. "Personally I think he's a taker."

"Got it." A "taker" was Mary Lee for a drug user who tried to con hospitals and clinics into giving them pain medication. They saw lots of them here, and—bless her heart—Mary Lee was always surprised.

Harper spotted him immediately. He didn't present as a methadone addict, but she recognized the symptoms of his drug use. Too skinny, brittle hair, slightly jaundiced. "Tell him we need his social security number."

Mary Lee smiled. They all knew the routine. She'd get his number, put the statistical database up on the computer monitor and type it in. The taker would see that, make some excuse to leave for a moment but never come back.

"Who else?"

They discussed the rest of the patients, but Harper kept looking back at Seth. No real reason to, just that something was off about him. She'd have to talk to him tonight, when they went shooting.

An hour later, she'd finished with another two patients and it was time for coffee. She headed for the break room but stopped as she saw Mr. Smith standing at the reception desk. Only, he wasn't looking at Mary Lee or the computer. His gaze was on Seth, and from the look on his face, he was concentrating hard.

Of course, Seth had put on his face prosthetics and he was wearing his baseball cap. So she was probably being paranoid. But the man just kept staring. Without saying a word, he turned and hurried out the door, and all her internal alarms went off.

She went to Seth and signaled him to follow.

Once they were alone in the break room, she shut the door. "Did you see that man at the reception area? He was in the dirty green T-shirt?"

Seth nodded.

"I think he may have recognized you."

Seth's posture changed. He straightened and got damn serious. "What makes you think so?"

"He was staring at you like he'd known you from high school, you know?"

"How long ago did he leave?"

"Just now."

Seth was out of the room so fast it made her jump, and by the time she got to the hallway he wasn't in sight. She had a pretty good idea where he would look for the guy—the post office. That's where his picture was, along with the other members of his Delta Force team.

She poured herself a cup of coffee, wondering if she could do anything to help. Call Nate? If Seth needed help, he had his cell phone. Try to find Smith herself? Whatever address he'd given Mary Lee would be false. They always were. So what could she do but wait?

SETH LOWERED HIS baseball cap as he headed in the direction of the post office. If Harper was right, he had to find this guy. Now. The question was, what was he going to do with him once he had him?

Kill him? An innocent civilian? Hold him hostage? Where? How? Shit.

He got his cell phone out of his back pocket and hit Nate's speed-dial number.

"Yeah?"

"Nate. I think I've been spotted."

Nate swore for a while as Seth crossed Broad Street. Three more blocks and he'd be at the post office. "What's his position?"

"Unknown, but I believe he's going to get the Wanted poster so he can be sure."

"You can't let him get to the police."

"What the hell am I supposed to do with him?"

"Can you get him back to the clinic?"

"How?"

"Use force if you have to. We'll meet you there."

"Then what?"

There was a long silence. "Just get him there."

Seth hung up and rounded Broad. There he was. Green shirt, dirty long hair. He was walking with a purpose and—just as Seth thought—he was headed to check out the poster.

Once the guy determined he'd found his man, he'd do one of two things—go right for the phone to call the cops or walk the two blocks to the police station. Seth's money was on the in-person visit. This was a junkie dreaming of reward money, and goddamned Omicron had made sure it was sizable. Enough to keep this junkie in drugs for a long time.

So when he reached the block with the post office, Seth headed for the second door—the exit that was closest to the police station.

There was a phone kiosk there, covered with graffiti and with only one functioning phone, but it would provide cover. Seth took off his jacket and put it over his left arm, then he pulled his shirt out of his pants. His cap came off next, which would make it harder for the guy to pick him out of the crowd.

He positioned himself at the one working phone, lifted the receiver off the hook and put it to his ear. He could see the exit and he calculated the distance he'd have to cover. Just past the door was an old apartment building with a covered entry. It wasn't the best place to take a prisoner, but it would do.

He hung up the phone and ran down the street, hoping the guy would wait the minute it took to get in position. He was sweating by the time he backed into the shadows. There would only be one chance, and the guy might just decide to yell his head off, which wouldn't end well for either of them.

He waited, his gun warming in his hand. The seconds ticked by, but Seth's whole universe had narrowed down to the few feet in front of him.

The guy stepped into view, and Seth grabbed him with his claw, pulling him into the shadows. He shoved his gun in his back, and the junkie's yelp cut short.

"You want to live, you walk with me. Quietly. You understand?"

"What if I don't want to?"

"Then I shoot you. I'm already wanted for treason. Murder wouldn't bother me in the least."

The guy turned to look at him. Seth guessed he seemed convincing, 'cause the guy just nodded.

With his jacket covering his right hand and his weapon, he urged the junkie onto the street, back toward the clinic. They passed a trash can, where the guy tossed the Wanted poster he'd taken from the post office wall.

He might be a junkie, but he wasn't stupid.

12

IF SETH DIDN'T COME back in five minutes, she was going to call Nate.

She'd practically chased everyone else out of the clinic—not that they were sorry to go, but it had terrified her to think of her staff being here if the police came.

As Harper downed her fourth cup of coffee, she tried to estimate how long it would take for her to walk to the post office and back. No matter how she figured, Seth had been gone too long. She put her cup down and noticed her hand shaking.

It couldn't all be going to hell now. Not after so much. Not when Seth was finding himself again. Becoming new. But what if Smith had gotten to the police? If they'd taken Seth into custody?

She wasn't naive enough to think there would be any good outcome. Omicron wouldn't let Seth live long enough to talk. And Smith would tell the cops where he'd spotted Seth, so they'd come here. She looked around her office. It may well be the last time she'd ever see it. Poor Mary Lee. Poor Karen. They'd all be grilled. And what could they say? That Harper had brought Seth to the clinic, that's what. That she and Seth lived together.

She'd never given anyone, including the clinic, her real address, but that didn't mean the police couldn't find her. Where would she go? The thought of leaving the only security she had made her want to weep. It wasn't even her house. She'd hated so much about it. And yet she couldn't bear to leave it.

A noise startled her, and she got to her feet, wishing she'd learned to shoot. She went into the hall and listened, but whatever she'd heard, it wasn't Seth. A quick trip back to her office, where she got her cell, then she went into the hall once more. She dialed Nate's number as she went to the back door.

He picked up on the first ring.

"Nate? Something's happened."

"I know."

"He called you?"

"Yeah. I'm on my way."

"He's been gone too long," she said. "I don't know what to do."

"I'll be there in five minutes," he said. "We'll figure it out."

"Wait," she said, seeing two men rounding the corner to the alley. "It's him. He's got the guy."

"Let me speak to him."

"In a minute," she said. "He's almost here."

She kept the phone to her ear, listening to the static-filled connection as Seth and Smith came closer. She could see now that Seth had his coat over his right arm, over his gun. Smith looked miserable and scared. She didn't blame him. She wouldn't want Seth as an enemy.

They walked around her old Ford, then came to the door. She held it open to let Smith pass. Her gaze went to Seth, so she didn't see Smith's move. He slammed into her, grabbing her by the shoulder, spinning her around so she was between Smith and Seth. Something sharp bit into her neck, and his arm squeezed her chest.

Seth swore as he lifted his gun, but she knew he wasn't going to shoot. His face told his story, and she was sure Smith read it clearly.

"Throw it," Smith ordered. "Throw it where I can see it go or I slice her throat."

"Okay," Seth said, his arms spreading wide. "Okay, don't hurt her."

"Throw it."

He did. Seth threw the gun to the ground, right by her front tire. "See? It's gone. Just don't hurt her. She didn't do anything."

Smith laughed, then coughed, but his grip never eased.

Harper's heart beat so fast she felt sure she was going to have a coronary. A trickle of blood slid down her throat as he pulled her back into the clinic.

She didn't want to go there. Once the door was closed, she knew he would do it. Slit her throat. Seth would watch her die and then he'd go after Smith.

"Wait," Seth said, taking one step forward.

Behind him, a car turned in the alley, then sped toward them. She looked, recognizing Nate behind the wheel of the pickup.

Too fast for her to understand, she was ripped away from Smith, thrown to the ground outside the door. When she could see again, Smith had the knife up and was lunging at Seth.

With a hoarse cry that made her gasp, Seth swung his claw in a roundhouse slam right into the side of Smith's head. It smashed hard, the sound like a melon dropped from the roof, followed by a guttural scream from Smith. Then he was on the ground, bleeding all over the back door welcome mat.

"Harper!"

Seth stood over her, his real hand on her arm, lifting her as he said her name again.

She found his eyes, round with panic. "I'm okay."

"Thank God."

By the time she was on her feet, Nate was there, lifting Smith's feet, dragging him into the clinic. A blood trail followed in an ugly swath, black and wet.

Seth got her moving, herding her toward the door. "We can't leave it like that," she said, staring at the blood.

"I'll take care of it. You just go inside."

She nodded, but he stopped her. Touched her neck with his fingertip. "He hurt you."

"I'm fine. It's nothing."

His lips tightened into white, but he let her go, following her closely as she went inside. He closed the door behind him.

Nate had dragged Smith halfway into exam one. She followed, knowing that Smith was dead. Wondering how she was going to explain any of this to the police.

She stopped when she saw that Nate had left him on the floor.

"You don't happen to have a body bag, do you?" he asked.

"We're a free clinic. If someone's that sick, we send them to the hospital."

He nodded, then looked behind her to Seth. "It's going to take me a while to get back. Are you two okay here?"

"We're fine," Seth said, looking at her instead of Nate. "We'll clean up." He turned to Nate and the body. "Do what you have to."

"Get some towels. Wrap his head."

Harper opened a cupboard above the sink where there were towels and paper gowns. She ignored the gowns but brought down all of the towels. Kneeling next to the body, she lifted the head and wrapped it as if she were applying a large bandage. "I still don't know how he—"

Nate touched her shoulder. "You took care of it. It's done."

Seth sighed behind her. "I didn't want to kill him."

"You did what was necessary." Nate rose and headed for the door.

"What are you going to do with him?" she asked.

"Nothing you need to know about."

"For the record," she said, "I hate this."

Nate gave her a sardonic smile. "You're not the only one." He headed out, socking Seth on the arm as he passed. Harper thought of football players, how they slapped each other after a touchdown. Surely, not even Nate could think of this as a winning play.

Seth watched Nate leave, then turned to Harper. He looked so concerned, as if he hadn't saved her.

He'd saved her. And she knew, just knew, that even without the prosthetic he would have killed Smith. Because Smith had hurt her.

She walked to Seth and he put his arms around her. She felt the heavy edge of his claw on one shoulder and the warmth of his real hand on the other. Mostly she felt safe. His chest was broad and hard, but when she laid her ear over his heart she could hear it beat with relief that she was all right.

Closing her eyes, she let the sound and the warmth seep inside. Her muscles relaxed and she breathed deeply, letting her own heart calm.

His lips touched the top of her head. The sweet innocence of the gesture made her eyes well with tears. It didn't matter. She wrapped her arms around his back and she rocked with him for a long time.

THEY DIDN'T GET TO the shooting range. At a quarter past midnight Seth opened the door to Harper's and held it for her as she walked inside.

She looked like hell. He didn't blame her. None of the night's events had been easy. Nate had ended up needing their help to dispose of the body. Seems Vince was meeting with a reporter, the kid who'd found Baker's body. So when Nate had come back with the body bag, it had been up to the three of them to load Smith up, get him into the back of the truck and take him to a field far from Boyle Heights.

Despite her all-business attitude, he knew she was bothered deeply by what they'd had to do. But he also knew she understood there was no choice. Now, after it was all over, after they'd buried the body where no one would find him and after the long drive home, she was starting to crumble.

"Come on," he said, taking her purse from her shoulder and putting it on the kitchen table. "We're almost done."

She looked up at him but couldn't really muster a smile. He guided her through the kitchen and down the hall. Once in her bedroom, he turned down the covers, then took her to the bathroom, where he undressed her as if she were a child.

She seemed bemused but unwilling to stop him.

For his part, it wasn't a chore. He took off her boots first, then her pants. She lifted her arms obediently when he took off her sweater. He tried not to be anything but helpful, but looking at her in her white bra and her blue bikini panties, he wanted to lose himself inside her. He wanted the oblivion of her body to take him away.

Instead he turned her around and with his one good hand he undid the clasp of her bra. She let it fall, then turned to him.

Her blond hair was a tangle and a smudge of dirt marred her pale cheek. So beautiful.

Unable to stop himself, he pulled her close, resting his head between her naked breasts.

She touched his head, then petted his hair, and he

closed his eyes. Although he wanted to stay right there forever, he moved back and reached for her panties.

"No," she whispered. "Stand up."

He obeyed, rocking slightly. Shit, he was as tired as she was.

"Now you," she said, tugging at his shirt.

He let her take it off, but when she went for the straps holding his wrist and hand, he stopped her. "Why don't you start the hot water."

She did, and while her back was turned he took off the claw and the wrist and the sock. After he'd kicked off his shoes and done the toe thing to get his socks off, she came back to him. Standing very close, she pulled his zipper down, the sound drowned out by the shower, then she undid his button.

He pushed his pants and shorts off while she pulled down her panties. Naked, she took his hand in hers and pulled him under the water.

First they washed. They shared the soap and the washcloth, scrubbing every part of their bodies hard. She washed his right shoulder, the places he could never reach. He washed her hair with his good hand. Finally they were clean and warm, and the stark reality of their awful night seemed far away. Until she touched his stump.

He jumped back as if she'd burned him and stared at the empty space at the end of his arm.

He'd killed a man tonight. "I killed him," he said softly.

"You saved me."

"I killed him with this. Not the metal."

"You saved me. He had a knife to my throat."

Seth nodded, but he wasn't really listening. He was trying to take it all in. He'd killed a man, and it wasn't because he was a trained soldier. That junkie had threatened Harper's life and he'd lost it. He'd come apart not because he was threatened but because she was. "I didn't think it would be like that."

"Like what?"

He looked at her, then back at his arm, so familiar until the wrist and then it was a blank. Erased. "It still feels like it's there. It hurts. It itches."

"It's been part of you your whole life." She touched the end of his stump. "It still has power. Whatever power you give it."

He gave her the best smile he could. "I'm supposed to be comforting you."

"You did. You are."

He pulled her close again, this time with both his right hand and his left arm. "Nate said Tam is at the last stage of development with the antidote. Once it's viable, things are going to change."

Harper laughed. "Yeah, it's going to get worse."

"Probably. But it'll also reduce the value of their gas. They're selling it as an ultimate weapon, one that can't be stopped. We're chopping them off at the knees."

"They'll get desperate. They'll try and sell everything they can before we can get the antidote out there."

"And we'll be all over them. The only thing that's going to end this is total exposure. What they created, why. And how they used taxpayer dollars to do it."

She sighed. "I don't to want think about it anymore."

He pulled back and looked at her face. So clean and beautiful. "It's not going away, Harper. And your life won't really be yours until we get them."

She took his face between her hands. "Here's what I know," she said. Then she kissed him. Long and deep. And the ploy worked—he didn't care about a damn thing except getting out of the shower and into bed.

Still kissing her, he reached behind to shut off the water. She pushed the door open and took him with her to grab a towel off the rack. He took another, and they dried each other just as they'd washed. When they'd stopped dripping, she headed toward the bedroom. He followed closely enough to get a ticket, but the tail he was gating was worth it.

"It's late," he said, climbing under the covers.

"Uh-huh."

"Don't you have to be at work early?"

"What part of *shut up* didn't you understand?"

"Bossy."

Her hand circled his half-erect cock. "You want to talk? Or…?"

He turned so he didn't dislodge her grip but he could still kiss her. "I pick *or.*"

She stroked as she kissed, getting him hard and ready. He returned the favor, stroking her outer lips, then, as he felt them swell, he slipped inside, finding her as hard as he was, only on a much smaller scale.

She wiggled beneath him, which made him even harder. Dr. Harper was the kind of woman you didn't mess with, and when she did something so girlie, it made him just a little bit crazy.

He rubbed her lightly, loving how her whole body reacted, her breasts on his chest, the smooth skin of her hip against his side. He wished he could touch her with both hands because she felt so damn good.

"Seth?" she said, her voice a breathy whisper.

"Yeah?"

"I really, really want you inside me."

"Do you now?"

She nodded. "Not that I don't love the foreplay, because I truly do, but right now I only want one thing."

He grabbed the other pillow from the top of the bed and put it next to her shoulder. She looked, smiled. Her hand left his cock to fold the pillow in half. He got to his knees and put his stump in position.

Like last night, she opened the condom and rolled it on him. Then she guided him home. And like last night, he lost whatever control he might have had the moment the tip slid against her moist opening.

She bucked up at the same moment he thrust, and his head nearly blew off at the incredible sensation.

He slammed into her again, and she pushed up, taking his bottom lip between her teeth. It hurt just enough, erasing the rest of the world.

But it was also faster. Just after she shuddered with her climax, he let go.

As the ringing in his ears dissipated, she touched his face. "Thank you."

"For what?"

"Everything. You're an amazing man. And when this is all over, when we've won, you're going to find an amazing woman who can appreciate you."

With that, she slipped away from him, curled up with her pillow and closed her eyes.

13

IT WAS EARLY, AND Seth hadn't had enough sleep, not by a long shot. Harper had awakened him at dawn. She'd touched his face with her fingertips. He'd kept his eyes closed, amazed that the feathery trace of her fingers across the bridge of his nose, down his cheek, across his lower lip, could make him want her so fiercely.

Yes, he knew exactly what he meant to her. There were no illusions about their time in bed. It didn't matter that he wanted more. This was what she offered, and God help him, he felt grateful she offered at all.

"I woke you," she whispered.

He pulled her close with his right arm. "You did."

"Sorry."

He opened his eyes. "I doubt it."

She smiled. "You're right. I'm not sorry. I want you too much to be sorry."

He pushed his hard cock into the warmth between her thighs. "You want this?"

She nodded.

He studied her face, stupidly hoping he'd see something there, something that would show him that her talk was just that. A defense, a lie. But all he saw was the truth.

"Hold that thought," she whispered, then she rolled out of his arms to reach for a condom on her bedside table. She was back in a flash, and before he could even think about telling her no, she prepared him with clinical efficiency. His dick got harder anyway.

"You want me on top?" she asked.

He grunted and got to his knees, straddling her waist. He took her right hand and pulled it over her head, pushing it into the pillow. Then he moved her left hand on top of it. His hand gripped both her wrists, holding her steady.

She looked up at him, but he couldn't read her eyes. The light was bleeding through the blinds, illuminating only her lips. He saw a glint of her teeth biting into her bottom lip.

Keeping his balance was tricky, but he used his one arm and his knees between her legs to get settled. He cursed the lack of his hand as he missed her opening once, twice, but then he sank deep into her wet heat.

She arched under him, squeezing him as he pulled almost all the way out. He made her wait there as he breathed deeply, adjusted his body to exactly the right position. When she bucked, he made her wait a few seconds more.

That was all he could stand. He slammed into her, just the way she liked it. No softness for Harper. No tenderness. Just the cock, as hard and as fast and as deep as he could go.

She writhed beneath him, and when the light moved higher on her face, he saw her eyes were closed and he hated her again. Not for cutting off his hand but for making him ache for something else he could never have.

He shut her out behind his own closed eyes and let his cock take over. A trickle of sweat moved down his spine. His hand shook while it held her steady. And then he came, pouring himself into nothing, into latex, not touching her. Not even making a mess.

He had no idea if she'd gotten off. And for once he didn't give a shit.

He was in the bathroom before she had a chance to say a word.

WHEN HARPER FINALLY opened her eyes, he was gone. She knew he was angry and she knew exactly why. She'd hurt his feelings, poor baby. But what the hell did he expect? Romance? Roses? A ring?

Didn't he get they weren't lovers? Hadn't she been really clear from the first? Surely, a guy like Seth knew that sex didn't mean anything.

So why was she still thinking about it? And why did she feel so goddamn empty inside? This had to end. The whole situation had gone from bad to worse. He was fine now, growing more and more capable with the prosthetic. If Nate couldn't take him in, then he'd just have to find someone who could.

SETH HAD DONE HIS workout because that wasn't negotiable. He'd also showered, made coffee, gotten dressed.

He hadn't put on the face putty because he wasn't going to the clinic. If a junkie could ID him, anyone could. He was just amazed that he hadn't been spotted earlier.

But he wasn't worried about someone seeing him. It was the opposite problem that had him staring at his cell phone. He'd been thinking about his folks since getting in the shower. No idea why. It wasn't a special day or anything like that. It was just a Wednesday. His dad would be at work by now. His mom would be doing something useful. Cleaning something, most likely. Damn, she loved that vacuum. She'd trained him better than the Army to keep his clothes and his bedroom neat. She'd never yelled at him if he screwed up. Oh, no. That would have been easier. She'd just sighed. Sighed and looked as if her heart would break. Over a T-shirt on the floor. Jeez.

He got up, poured himself another cup of coffee, then went back to the table. To the cell phone. It was a clean phone, couldn't be traced. Even if someone heard a whole conversation, they wouldn't be able to pinpoint where the call had come from.

So what would be the harm? Omicron knew he was alive. His parents knew he was alive. The only thing no one knew was where he was. So if he called and didn't say, there would be no problem.

He picked up the cell and dialed the number. Stared at it on the tiny LED screen. But he didn't press the send button.

If he called his parents and Omicron knew it, what would they do? Would they step up their surveillance?

Would they put pressure on his folks in hopes he would call again? Would those bastards hurt his parents to try and flush him out?

He put the phone down. He couldn't take the risk. Omicron would go to any lengths to get them all, and using his parents was right up their alley.

He drank some coffee, thought about calling Nate and finding out the plan for the day. Instead he called his parents' number.

His hand shook as he listened to the rings. On the third, he heard his mother say, "Hello?" He squeezed his eyes shut, listening for another word, any other word. Because she sounded just the same. Perpetually surprised that someone would call. Nice to everyone, even the most obnoxious salesman.

"Hello?"

It felt as if his chest was going to implode. He had to clench his teeth so he wouldn't speak. But maybe she could sense that it was him. That he was sorry. That everything was going down the toilet.

"Oh, for heaven's sake."

That was it. His mother hung up.

He'd kept her safe. In the dark. He turned off the phone and put it back down on the table.

HARPER STAYED IN THE shadow of the door. She tightened her robe, ran a hand over her hair. Should she go to him? Should she walk in and pretend she hadn't seen? It was early. She should probably just go back to bed. But bed had no appeal.

She had a pretty good idea who he'd tried to call. He actually missed his parents. Loved them. While she couldn't really empathize, she could understand his pain. She'd lost people, too. No one as close as a mother. Well, the truth was, she had lost her mother and her father, but that had happened long before she'd gone overseas.

What must it have been like for Seth? Growing up with a family who really cared? Who loved him unconditionally?

That's where her imagination failed. Her family—if one could bastardize the word—had taught her a few things, and none of them were about love. She had no idea where her mother was. Her father? He was in jail, where he belonged.

But still, she felt badly for Seth. He'd lost an awful lot. And now he didn't even have the clinic. No wonder he wanted hearts and roses with her. It was a damn shame that he'd have to go. She'd liked having him here.

She hadn't had a nightmare for two whole nights. Even with all that they'd been through, she'd slept. It was selfish, she knew, but having him next to her in bed was—

He stood up, and she backed into the hallway. The last thing she wanted to do was have a confrontation now. Seth wouldn't want her to see he'd been crying. Besides, she should get in the shower. She wanted to be at work before anyone else. Just to make sure everything looked normal.

NATE DIDN'T GO INTO the bus station. He waited by a small taco stand called Kan Kun, which was closed at six in the morning. It was also one and a half blocks from the Greyhound depot where Cade Huston was scheduled to arrive.

It had been a long time since Nate had seen his friend. Cade had come back from Kosovo and gone almost immediately to Colorado. He'd been missed.

Nate got out of the truck. He walked to the back, although he knew there was nothing there that would indicate what they'd used it for last night. His breath came out in crystalline puffs, and the cold bit sharply into his exposed skin, but he couldn't sit. Cade should be walking down the street any minute. He'd been on a bus for three days, and they hadn't spoken. All Nate knew was that somehow Cade had come out alive.

Almost ten minutes later Nate recognized the rolling gait of his friend. Cade was a big sucker. Six-four and built like a tanker. He'd been fierce even in training. Nate had been there when Cade had gone on a solo twenty-two-mile hike over incredibly rough terrain, only to find that Cade had broken his foot on mile two. He just never gave up. When Nate had been given the choice of men for his team, Seth had been first, Cade a close second.

Half a block away, Cade broke into a jog. They came together in a brutal hug, comrades, alive when there was no reason they should be.

Nate stepped back to look at his friend, anonymous in his big Army coat. He'd worn jeans and sturdy boots, carried a small duffel and looked as if he hadn't slept in days. "You look like shit, my man."

"Look who's talking."

"You hungry?"

"I'm always hungry."

"Let's go."

Cade threw his duffel in the truck, then got in beside Nate, who drove to a diner near downtown. They went inside and took a seat in the back, far from prying ears.

"So what the hell happened?" Nate asked after they'd gotten their coffee.

"Six days ago, someone hit a trip wire three clicks from the cabin. The good part was that everything worked like it was supposed to. I had my cameras mounted and my radar. I saw them approach."

"How many?"

"I stopped counting at ten and got my ass out of there."

"You used the tunnel."

Cade nodded. "I did. There was no time to salvage much. All I could really take was the tapes." He shrugged.

Nate knew how much he was leaving out. He could well imagine the terror of getting through that tunnel. The dark, the cold. Knowing any second he could be found.

"It went up like a Roman candle. The whole damn place. I was a mile away and I was knocked to the ground by the percussion."

"Shit."

"Like I said, it went like it was supposed to. All but the part where I screwed up."

"I never would have guessed they'd wire your grandfather."

Cade shook his head, clearly troubled by his mistake. "It was indulgent and stupid. I'm just sorry the cost was so high."

Nate shook his head. "Forget it. It's history. I'm just glad to see you here, buddy. We need a man like you on the front lines."

"Hell, I'd just like to find a safe place to sleep."

"It's not fancy, but you can stay with me, at least for the time being."

"You want to fill me in on the current situation?"

"Later. Seth is coming by this afternoon, and we'll give you the details. For now, let's chow down and then you get some rest. You're gonna need it."

Cade stretched his hand across the table and Nate took hold of it. No one who hadn't served could know what it meant to meet a team member after an operation. That they were all still alive was a miracle. He wondered, squeezing his friend's hand, how long this state of grace would last.

WHEN SHE PARKED THE car behind the clinic, Harper's gaze went right to the spot where Smith had fallen. She expected to see the stain of blood, but there was nothing left of him. Or the welcome mat. Of course, if someone was really looking, they'd find traces. But who was there to tell? Was there anyone out there who would wonder what happened to the dead man? Even if she'd wanted to find a connection, they didn't know his name, his age, anything about him except that he'd been desperate and that he'd kept a knife in the lining of his coat.

She knew that there had been no options. Smith had been beyond reason, and when he'd drawn blood, even though it had been that tiny trickle, he'd signed his own death warrant. The tragedy was that if he hadn't been so sharp, hadn't seen through Seth's disguise, he'd be alive today.

What kind of life was another matter. Not one she was prepared to debate, not even with herself.

She got out of the car, locked it behind her and walked slowly to the door. She'd helped clean up inside, but Seth had taken care of this area. He'd used his janitor's bucket and soap, and she supposed he'd gotten pretty good at cleaning in the last few weeks.

Her hand trembled as she unlocked the door. Once she inspected exam one, she'd be fine. She would. She'd seen her share of death, more than most. As a doctor, especially in a war zone, she'd witnessed the most horrible of mutilations, the most senseless waste of human lives. Nothing could compare to the deaths in Serbia. And yet this junkie who'd almost killed her was making her shake like a rookie.

Maybe it wasn't Smith's death that had her so rattled. Maybe it was how close they'd come to being caught. She remembered the panic she'd felt when Seth was late. Dammit. She'd tried so hard to separate herself from the team. She should never have been part of their damn *team*.

She closed the door behind her and turned on the hall lights. The floor looked pristine, at least for that floor. It was old and cracked and it should have been replaced years ago, but there was no sign of blood or even scuff marks.

The short walk to exam one took all her will, but when she turned on that light, the room was as clean as the hallway. Mary Lee, the others, they'd never suspect anything out of the ordinary.

She left the room and went all the way back to the break room. In the quiet, she carefully prepared the first pot of coffee, watching the slow drip as it filled the carafe.

Her thoughts had gone back to that day, the day that had changed it all. She'd been in her apartment, a UN building close to the hospital in the center of Kosovo. Banging on her door had awakened her, and her first thought was that Tanja was having her baby. She was a nurse at the hospital, very skilled, and her English had been terrific, and she was overdue. But standing on her doorstep was Jelka, a young aide who was still studying to get into university.

She was a pretty girl with long, dark hair and thick dark brows. Her panic was clear from the moment Harper had opened the door. Something was wrong in her village. No one was answering the phones. Not her parents, not her aunt or her cousins. Something was wrong, would the doctor come?

It had never occurred to Harper to say no. She'd gotten dressed, grabbed her kit and they'd headed out of Kosovo in an old Jeep.

The coffee stopped dripping, and Harper poured herself a cup. As predicted, she'd stopped shaking. The important thing now was to stop thinking. To fill herself with another task, something that wouldn't take her back to the horror of that day.

She wished there were patients in the waiting room. But they wouldn't start lining up for at least an hour. The only thing she could do was bury herself in paperwork.

Walking back to her office, she wondered what Seth was doing. She hadn't asked and he hadn't volunteered. Frankly she didn't want to know.

He'd surprised her, she could admit that now. She'd never had a very high opinion of Army types, finding most of them dull and proud, an odd combination that rubbed her the wrong way. But Seth, he wasn't like that at all.

Admittedly most of the time he'd been with her he'd been angry and depressed. But she'd seen his spirit and his honor, and he had never been dull.

None of them were. Not Nate or Boone or Cade. They were bright and capable and fiercely patriotic. She supposed that's why they'd been recruited into Delta. They truly were the best and the brightest. So why had they been trapped in this nightmare?

She'd found it by mistake, a luck of the draw, but these men had been actively tricked by the people they'd sworn to protect with their lives. It made no sense. Not any of it.

Work, she had to work. To get her head away from the thought of losing Seth. Damn him for his sentimentality. The house would feel so empty. And so would her bed.

She was right to make sure he understood there was

nothing between them but the sex. Nothing to look forward to, nothing to count on. Because it was the truth.

"AH, A MAN WITH discriminating taste."

Seth looked behind him, where a girl with one ring in her nose and another in her lower lip was nodding, making her spiky hair bounce. She also had a tattoo on her shoulder, a flaming heart, which was made prominent by her tube top. He had his coat on but was still chilled from his walk. He wondered if they made her wear the skimpy top or if she just didn't feel the cold.

"That's an original," she said, pointing at the design he'd been looking at. "Not mine. My boss's. He's a genius."

"I can see that," Seth said, although he wasn't very up on the art of tattoo. He'd wandered in here mostly because he was just killing time, but once he'd started looking around, he'd been intrigued.

Of course he knew a bunch of guys with tats. It was almost regulation in the Army, especially with Special Forces. But he'd never been tempted. It just seemed so permanent.

Now that his life expectancy was measured in hours, the idea appealed. Especially where he wanted it.

"Were you thinking about it for your…you know?"

"My stump?"

She nodded. "We've done a bunch of amputees here. Mostly ex-military. They always want their insignias and stuff. Did you lose your hand in Iraq?"

"No."

"Oh."

She crossed her arms and he saw she had painted her nails black. He couldn't help but wonder about her parents. He doubted she was even eighteen. Were they tattooed themselves? Or appalled at their daughter's rebellion? If his kids ever tried anything like that…

What was he thinking? He wasn't going to have any kids. "Is your boss here?"

"Yeah." She looked behind her to a door covered by a black curtain. "He's still setting up."

"How much would something like this cost?"

"That one's about fifty bucks."

"Whoa."

"It's worth it. Seriously, look at the detail."

He did. It was a black dragon, but his wings were torn and damaged, as if he'd just come out of a long, bloody battle. "I don't know. How long does it take to heal?"

"You'd have to wear a bandage for, like, three days. Put some antiseptic over it. The only other thing is not to soak it for a month. It's not bad."

"Fifty bucks, huh?"

She nodded.

"How long would it take?"

"Couple of hours."

He couldn't stay that long. He had to be at Nate's in an hour and he had to get there by cab. His car had been wrecked, and left, along with his hand, on a road in Sunland.

No way there was enough money for this. "I'll think about it," he said.

"Wait, I'll give you a card."

She walked over to a small desk in the corner, giving him a good view of the tat just above her butt. Nice.

He tucked the card in his coat pocket, then headed out again. No other store on the street was half as interesting. Except for the bakery. He had enough for a coffee and a danish, which he took with him.

As he walked, he thought about what Harper had said last night. This morning, rather. How she'd said he'd make someone a great husband. And he wondered again why she'd said it.

She seemed determined to let him know that she wasn't interested in him. His dick, yes, but nothing more. Why make the point so clear, so often? Was it going to be shoved in his face every time they made love?

He laughed. They hadn't made love. They'd had sex. Which clearly wasn't all he'd wanted, was it? If it was all about sex, he wouldn't have given a shit what she'd said. But her words had bothered him all day.

He had no clue what he wanted from Harper. Maybe nothing. But maybe more.

14

SHE'D SEEN TWO PATIENTS, both of whom were repeat visitors, and both of them had asked her if she was all right. The fact was, she wasn't all right, not even close.

Instead of getting better, the day had gone straight downhill. She'd spilled her coffee when Mary Lee had walked into the break room unexpectedly. She'd almost stuck herself with a needle. And, dammit, she couldn't stop from going to reception to see who was in the waiting room. Even if someone was there from Omicron, did she expect them to be wearing a sign? Was every man in a suit secretly in the CIA and out to kill her?

It was crazy and she hated it. All she'd ever wanted was to be left alone, and now she felt as if every eye in the world was on her, every motive nefarious. Would the police come arrest her for murder? Or harboring a traitor? Would Omicron poison her coffee? Kill everyone in the clinic?

She wished for the hundredth time that she'd never gone to Kosovo. That she'd never agreed to escape. And, God knows, she shouldn't have agreed to put the trauma room in her house.

Nothing was worth this kind of fear. She'd never willingly betray the others, but she had to get out of this. The others, they were soldiers and used to living in a state of terror and uncertainty. This was never how she'd planned her own life. All she wanted was to be a doctor, to have her own home, to not be obligated to a living soul.

Everything had been relatively okay until Seth. Yeah, he was good in bed, but so were a whole bunch of other guys. Guys who didn't know how to kill with one blow to the head. If Seth disappeared, she wouldn't be much of a target. She really didn't know anything, as far as they were concerned. She was a doctor who'd seen a village wiped out by a chemical agent. It could have been any number of agents, none of which would make her suspicious.

Everything would be normal again once Seth left.

"Dr. Douglas?"

"Hmm?"

"Are you okay, honey?"

She put on her most reassuring smile. "Thanks, Mary Lee, but don't worry. I've just got a lot on my mind."

"You'd tell me if something was wrong, wouldn't you?"

"I would."

"For example, if you were thinking about the whereabouts of a certain young man?"

Harper realized she had been standing in the middle of the break room for several minutes, empty coffee cup in hand. And then she realized that Mary Lee was referring to Seth and that everyone in the clinic must have come to the conclusion that they were lovers.

She felt her face heat as she went to the coffeepot and poured another cup, even though she'd originally come to wash the cup and get some water.

She'd worked so hard to keep her private life private. Then Seth had walked into the picture, and even this place was now unsafe. "Seth is fine, Mary Lee. He's just out looking for another job. And, no, we're nothing more than friends."

"Friends," Mary Lee repeated. "Pardon me for saying, but the way he looks at you? That's not one friend to another."

"I have no control over how anyone looks at me. But I can assure you the looks are not returned."

"Uh-huh," the receptionist said but in a way that was so disbelieving that Harper felt slapped.

What had happened here? A month ago, no one in this place would have dared be so familiar with her. God, everything had gone to hell while she wasn't looking.

"Is my next patient ready?"

"Yes, Dr. Douglas. She's in exam one."

At the mere mention of the room, Harper tensed, and—dammit all to hell—her hand was shaking again. "Thank you." She left the room as quickly as she could and went straight into her office.

Once the door was shut and locked, she went into her purse and pulled out the cell phone Nate had given her. She dialed his number and waited impatiently for him to pick up.

"Yeah?"

"Nate? It's Harper."

"Hey, how you doing? Seth's here if you—"

"No," she said, interrupting him. "I don't want to speak to him. I want you to tell him to come get his things. I don't think he should stay with me. In fact, I know he shouldn't. I want him out before I get home."

"Did something happen? Were you threatened?"

"No. I'm fine. Or I will be as soon as he's gone. Just do that, okay? And know that if someone gets hurt, I'll do what I can, but no one stays with me again or the whole deal is off."

"Harper—"

She cut him off, then turned the phone off altogether. She didn't care to have a discussion about her decisions. All she wanted was to get her life back—and she wasn't about to wait for the fall of Omicron to do it.

NATE CURSED THE WOMAN under his breath as he severed the connection. Behind him, Seth, Cade, Kate and Vince were sitting on his ratty couch. They'd been discussing the plans for Tam's experiment. It had felt damn good, like old times. In fact, not ten minutes ago he'd gotten off the phone with Boone, who'd had some luck in Nevada. He was pretty sure he knew where Omicron was manufacturing the gas. Nate had figured the phone call was Boone again. Instead it had been a body blow to his closest friend.

Seth had clearly gotten that all was not well with Harper. Just the fact that she hadn't wanted to speak to him was ominous. Nate knew the man wasn't prepared to hear his message. But there was no out.

"She okay?" Seth asked.

"Physically, yeah. I don't think she's doing so well emotionally, though."

Seth sat up straighter, then decided that wasn't good enough and he stood. "What did she say?"

Nate went close, but he didn't touch Seth. "Why don't we go in the other room?"

"Why don't you just tell me what she said?'

"She wants you to get your stuff out of the house."

"She's kicking me out?"

Nate nodded.

"That's not even her fucking house."

"It is, Seth. What are you going to do? Stay there against her wishes?"

Seth cursed and went to the window. Nate didn't have a clue what to do. If this had just been a woman Seth had been seeing, he would have told his friend to blow it off. But it was Harper, and she was still a necessary part of the team. From what Nate could see, there was a lot going on between them that could end up endangering them all. "Why don't you let her cool off for a couple of days. Then talk to her. I'm sure this is just the fallout from last night."

"You don't know that," Seth said. "She didn't want me there from the beginning. I'm sure she regrets not letting me die."

"Seth, that's not true." Kate got up and went to him, although Nate could see from Seth's body language that he didn't want her advice. "Harper's not used to any of this. She's had trouble with this from the very start. Remember, she's not military."

"Neither are you."

"But I've been around you guys a lot more. Nate's right. You need to give her some time."

"Time. Right." Seth headed for the front door and slammed out.

"Think he'll be coming back anytime soon?" Vince asked. He took Kate's hand as she sat down next to him. She gave him a worried look and a small shake of the head.

"He'll catch up." Nate sat down in the folding chair at the small table where he'd kept his notes, then turned back to Vince. "Now what were you saying about that reporter?"

"He wants to come tomorrow night."

"He's a security risk. We can't have him there."

"I think we need to consider it," Vince said. "He's risking his life on this story. He wants to have some proof, something real to back him up when he goes to the editor."

Nate shook his head. "How old is he?"

"Twenty-three. He's a believer, don't get me wrong. But he's not Corky Baker and he needs more to substantiate what he's writing."

"How can we give him that? If he lets on that Tam is alive…"

"He won't. He understands what's at stake."

"Okay, but you're in charge of him, Vince," Nate said. "If it all goes to hell, I'm blaming you."

Vince grinned. "Been there, done that. I'll watch him, don't worry about it."

"There isn't anything about this operation that doesn't worry me." Nate rubbed his face and wished he could sleep for about two weeks. "Kate, do me a favor. Give Harper a call. See what you can do."

"I'll try, but don't count on me to come through. I don't know her very well."

"You've got the best shot of any of us."

Kate leaned into Vince's shoulder. "Damn rotten timing for them to have a lover's spat."

Nate shook his head. What was it with everyone that they had to pick now to fall in love? Didn't they realize their chances of coming out of this alive were about fifty to one? Dopes. "Okay, let's talk about living arrangements. Now that we have one more body to worry about."

HARPER WALKED INTO the empty house and saw immediately that Seth had done as she'd asked. His mug was gone from its usual spot beside the coffeepot.

A lump came to her throat, but she swallowed it down. She would not get sentimental about this. She'd made the right decision. He was a great guy and all, but he was dangerous. Too dangerous.

What she needed now was some peace and quiet. It had been such a long time since she'd had her own life. Could she even remember what it was like to live on her own? To not wonder what he was doing? If he was in pain? What kind of crap he was going to give her?

She never should have kept him here. Like a stray dog, he'd insinuated himself into her life, and that wouldn't do. Even if the Omicron thing was over tomorrow, she would still want her privacy and her freedom.

She dropped her purse off on the kitchen table, then

headed for her bedroom. The bed was made, and she hadn't left it that way this morning. Pulling back the comforter, she saw Seth had changed the sheets. Probably washed them, too. It must have been some trick for him to put on the new linens with his claw.

Changing clothes quickly, she put on a pair of jeans and an old sweater, then she went down the hall to the basement door. Her steps echoed as she descended the stairs, and, yep, he'd cleared out of there, too.

One thing she had to say for the guy—he sure knew how to clean. He'd probably learned that in the Army, not the clinic. She supposed it didn't really matter.

She walked around the room, her fingers grazing the sparkling stainless steel. He hadn't left a print behind, let alone something more substantial. It was as if he'd never been there.

Except she remembered. How horribly sick he'd been when the infection had hit the remains of his hand. How it had been so touch and go. The final decision that she alone was qualified to make. How scared she'd been to do the surgery by herself, wishing she could send him to a hospital, where he belonged.

And, oh, how he'd hated her. Funny how hard that had been to recall these last few weeks. But when he'd woken with his hand gone, he'd wished her a thousand curses. Every look had been a glare, every word a slur.

That really hadn't bothered her. He'd like to think so, she was sure, but she'd been around too many people in similar situations to take it personally.

If he'd stayed mad at her, she probably wouldn't

have minded keeping him here. But things had changed. One day she was the devil, the next a lover.

She hugged her waist, remembering how it had been with him, how he'd just wiped her out. And how comforting to feel his hard body right next to her when she went to sleep.

She climbed the stairs again, trying to keep her footsteps quiet, but in the empty, sterile room, the sound bounced off the walls. It was better upstairs, on the hardwood floor.

She was a little hungry but not enough to really cook anything. She went to the fridge and grabbed a carton of yogurt. Then she went to the living room, which they'd hardly ever visited. She turned on the TV, not at all sure what was on. She'd lost track of the series and she didn't pay for cable. She ended up turning the damn thing off after a few rounds with the remote.

She could read. Hadn't she been complaining that she had no time for books anymore?

On the other hand, maybe she should just crawl into bed. Tomorrow was the street fair, where she and Mary Lee would hand out condoms. Their booth never got that much action, but the waiting around was harder on her than if they'd been swamped. She'd never done well with idle time.

She finished off her yogurt, threw the carton away, then went back to her bedroom. It was dark already, and she was so exhausted she'd probably fall asleep immediately. So she changed once more, this time into her sleep shirt.

In the bathroom, she stopped short. There was a note taped to the mirror. She thought about throwing it out without a glance, but she wasn't quite up to that.

Harper—
I don't understand. I thought that it was good between us, even if you never wanted anything more than sex. You never asked my opinion, so I never gave it. I would have been okay with just that, if that's all you wanted to offer. What I don't get is that I thought we were friends. I know the recent events have been hard, but that's when friends are most necessary.

  Anyway, don't take any risks, okay? I know you don't want to be involved, but you are. They'll come after you if they can. So keep low and stay alert.
Seth

She crumpled the paper in her fist and threw it in the trash can. He just didn't get it and she doubted he ever would. Which was fine. Because she didn't need any friends. She'd been just fine on her own and she would be again. Pity about the sex, but oh, well. The price was too high. He'd see that in the end.

She brushed her teeth and washed her face, then crawled into her big bed. As expected, she fell asleep in minutes.

WHAT SHE HADN'T expected was to wake at three-thirty from a nightmare. She'd been back in Serbia, of course, but this time she'd come to the village when everyone there had still been alive.

She'd watched the children play—the little boy with his truck, the girl with her curly-haired doll. She'd seen the townspeople go about their daily chores—putting out the garbage, buying bread and cheese. And then the plane had come over them and the choking had begun. No scent, no plume. Invisible death stealing every vestige of life, including her own.

She'd struggled and coughed and felt her insides churn. There was no voice to scream for help as everyone around her fell to the ground in their own individual agonies. As she'd fallen on a pile of bodies, she'd awakened with a gasp.

Tears flowed down her cheeks, and she reached across the bed for Seth.

He wasn't there. No one was there. Just like her death in her dream, she was alone. So alone it felt like the end of the world.

15

To CALL IT A FESTIVAL was truly a joke. Harper came here every month, to the little booth they put up right next to the CVS Pharmacy parking lot. The clinic's booth usually had a sunglasses vendor next door, but from time to time they got lucky and the falafel cart would be there instead. They got more traffic with falafel than sunglasses. Although they never really got a great many people to come by. Usually horny guys hoping to get lucky. Every once in a while they got someone serious, a young girl perhaps too shy to go to her mother's gynecologist but who didn't want to get pregnant. No one ever brought up the topic of HIV on their own. Somehow all of these young people felt immune, as if nothing bad could ever happen to them. Except that every day someone else in this neighborhood contracted HIV or was killed in a drive-by shooting. The gangs here were notorious, but that was true in most big cities.

All they could do was try, which they did. It was typically her and Mary Lee, although sometimes some of the other doctors or nurses would come by for a few hours. Regardless, Harper showed up. She stayed in the booth, usually with a book in hand, and waited for someone to stop. Some days she read the whole book without getting out of her chair.

Today was one of those quiet days, probably because it was miserably cold, with a sharp breeze that seeped right down to the bones. Neither sunglasses nor falafel had braved the weather, which was probably wise. Harper doubted she'd save a life today.

Mary Lee hummed a song she'd learned in church as she puttered with the flyers. A very large box of condoms in brightly colored wrappers rested in a big round tub they'd bought at a flea market.

Harper tried to read. It wasn't easy, though, because every few seconds she looked up, sure someone was watching her. Someone from Omicron, who would try to kill her and hit Mary Lee by mistake. When she wasn't looking up, she was debating the wisdom of working at the clinic at all.

Was it fair to her friends, her colleagues, to put them in such danger? What if Smith hadn't been the one to die? What if it had been her? Or Seth? Smith could have hurt anyone with that knife of his. And he was nothing compared to Omicron. They were CIA with high-tech weapons and highly trained men. They'd already proven they had no morals. They killed because they could.

She shook the thoughts away, then tried to read again. Three words later, the hair on the back of her neck stood up. She tried not to be obvious about staring, but it was dark and dreary and there were so many shadows.

It was no use. There were too many places a person

could hide, especially if they were peering through a high-powered rifle lens. She'd find a replacement. Quit. The problem was she couldn't even get another job, because that would just shift the danger. How would she survive? No money, no friends, certainly no family to turn to.

She looked down the street to the park bench by the pawnshop. A homeless man huddled there, clutching his shopping cart. Was that her destiny? To live on the streets, afraid every moment for the rest of her life?

She wished Seth were here. No, she hadn't changed her mind—he was too dangerous to truly want back. But she missed the illusion of safety.

The illusion was really all she required, because, in truth, that was all anyone had. A bus could hit her tomorrow. She could trip and fall and crack her head open. As long as she could clutch the illusion to her chest, she could manage life. It's what she loved most about the clinic. She'd felt safe there, useful and immune from anything out in the world. How could she give that up? How could she walk away from what had truly given her life meaning?

She wondered what Seth was doing. How much he hated her for throwing him out like that. He must, despite the words on the note. God, sometimes her own capacity to be a bitch shocked her down to her toes.

She had no business treating Seth so poorly. He'd saved her life. He'd saved her nights. He'd been there for her in every respect.

And how had she rewarded him? She'd tossed him out like so much garbage.

It was for the best. Eventually he would have discovered this side of her, and the longer she played the nice doctor, the more hurt he would have been once he realized she wasn't nice in any way.

It wasn't all selfishness. She had to believe that.

"Dr. Douglas," Mary Lee said, "it's time for lunch. Would you like to go or should I pick it up?"

"What would you prefer?"

"I think a walk would do me good."

"That's fine, thanks."

"I was toying with the notion of a burger. How does that sound?"

"Great." Harper reached behind her chair for her purse and she pulled out a twenty. "That should take care of everything."

"You don't have to do that, you know."

"It's my pleasure. Honestly."

Mary Lee, who was the single mother of four boys, took the bill with a smile and a nod. "Fries?"

"Oh, yeah."

"Caramel milk shake? Thin?"

"You know me too well."

"I don't hardly know you at all." Mary Lee got her small red purse from behind the counter and headed out the back of the booth. She touched Harper's shoulder with her slender brown hand.

Harper watched her walk down the street, and even the thought of Mary Lee getting hurt was enough to make her sick to her stomach.

She couldn't ask him to come back. Not ever.

THE PLAN HAD BEEN looked at every way from Sunday, and still, Nate wasn't happy with it. He'd found the perfect lab for Tam's experiment. It belonged to an insecticide manufacturer, one who also rented it out to local colleges and universities for experiments much like the one Tam planned to run tonight. They had a cloud chamber there, and she'd be able to measure the viability of the antidote after prolonged exposure to air and pollutants. When he'd told her about it, she'd been delighted. But he was less so.

He and Seth had cased the place early this morning, and there was no question the alarm system could be disarmed. What bothered Nate was the location—too close to civilization and traffic for his taste—and the guards that policed the perimeter.

He didn't want anyone to get hurt. For that to happen, Tam had exactly two hours to complete her tests, and she'd said that would be tight. Very tight. Even worse, when the test was running, there was no way to disguise the noise. If the patrol came by, they were toast.

And then there was the matter of Eli. Vince had been convincing. Nate just hoped the kid knew what the hell he was doing.

"Where's Seth?"

He turned to Cade, who'd slept a good deal of the morning away. He'd needed it. "He had some errands. I lent him the truck."

"Okay." They were in Nate's place, in what he laughingly referred to as a living room. Most people would call it a closet. "What weapons are we using tonight?"

Nate sat down on the ratty couch. No one knew more

about guns than Cade. Tonight would require all the expertise they could get.

THE MAN'S FACE WAS hidden from view by his coat, the hood pulled tightly to obscure his features. Harper put her book down and looked for an easy escape route, but the way the booth was set up, it was awkward. The car was all the way across the parking lot, and she didn't want to leave the booth with Mary Lee still getting lunch.

With her heart racing and her mouth suddenly dry, she stood as the man got nearer. Something shifted as he crossed the street. She recognized his gait, the broad shoulders. It wasn't Omicron at all.

Her gaze went to his left side, to his arm, but his hand, his claw, was obscured by his coat. Still, she knew it was Seth.

Anger rose in her so quickly she could hardly breathe. What the hell was he doing here? Hadn't the clinic been enough for him? Did he have to bring trouble to this place, too?

He walked up to the booth, his gaze moving over her face as if he hardly knew her.

She went to the counter. "What are you doing here?"

He shrugged carelessly, but his eyes were concerned as hell. Worried.

She hated that he wasn't as scared as she felt. "You have to go."

"What?"

"Get out. Wasn't my message clear enough? I don't

want you coming near the clinic or my house or here. Especially not here. Mary Lee is due back any minute."

"I thought we should talk."

She closed her eyes, willing her heart to stop beating so fast. "There nothing to say."

"I can't even ask what the hell happened? Was it Smith? I didn't want him to die."

"But he did. And he almost killed me. What if it hadn't been an early night? What if...?"

"What if what? It happened. It's real. So is Omicron. And so is the danger you're in."

She shook her head. "No. I was fine until you showed up. No one bothered me. I changed my name, moved to that stupid house. I was fine."

"What about the nightmares? You think waking up every night in a cold sweat is fine?"

She took in a deep breath and let it out slowly. "Look, just forget it, okay? It's not personal. You were great, you rocked my world. But I can't have you here."

He looked at her with disbelief for a long moment. Then he leaned closer. "Not personal? I don't think it can get any more personal. We slept together. We've been through hell together. What's more personal than that?"

"How we make it through. I'm not a fighter, Seth. I'm not like you."

"Bullshit. You're a warrior if I ever saw one. You use a scalpel instead of a gun, sure, but I've been there when it's been hard. You never flinched."

"Are you kidding? I can't move without being scared to death. I might have to quit the only thing that keeps me grounded because I don't want everyone at the clinic to be killed. I want nothing more than to have it all disappear."

"Including me."

She felt an ache bloom in her chest that made it hard to breathe. "Including you."

"I can help."

"No, you can't. You brought death to my door, Seth."

"Me? You think I wanted any of this? I'd like it all to go away, too. But there's nothing I can do about how I got here. Only what I'm going to do from this moment on."

"Right. Because you're a soldier. I'm not. I never should have been involved in this mess."

"And the rest of us? You don't give a damn about Kate or Tam?"

"I barely know them. I barely know you."

"Tell yourself whatever you need to about the others, but don't try and tell me you don't know me."

"What, we spent a few months together and now we're soul mates? We didn't pick each other, Seth. We had no choice."

"There's always a choice. Yesterday you made yours. I made mine a long time ago."

"What's that supposed to mean?"

"Nothing. Forget it."

"What choice did you make?"

"I'm going to fight the war that needs winning."

"So, I'm a coward."

"No. You're just kidding yourself."

She turned from him. Out of the corner of her eye she saw Mary Lee walking back from the diner, a big paper bag in her arms. Behind Mary Lee she saw a truck, one that looked awfully familiar. "How long have you been here?"

"Does it matter?"

"Yes, it does."

"Since you set up."

She turned back to face him. "Why?"

"Because you're vulnerable here."

"I've been vulnerable since I came back from Kosovo."

He shrugged again. "It's just as important to know what wars don't need fighting," he said. He looked her in the eyes, and what she saw there made the ache ten times worse. Then he turned and left, moments before Mary Lee walked into the booth.

THE NIGHT WAS MORE miserable than the day had been, and Nate figured that was one in their favor. With any luck, the security patrol would want to stay in their vehicles with the windows rolled up against the evening chill.

He was at the back door to the lab with Tamara and Eli behind him. All of them were dressed in black, invisible against the night. With Seth's help, he'd disarmed the alarm system and was now opening the door. If their luck held, all would be quiet. If not...

The door swung open, and he hurried his charges inside. He could tell Eli wanted to rush in but held himself back until Tam entered.

Nate closed and locked the door behind himself, then turned on his flashlight. He knew the building now, all through schematics, though, so he supposed some things had changed. It was a pretty sure bet, however, that no one was going to move the big stuff like the cloud chamber.

With the two of them close on his heels, he went through the offices to the back of the building, where there was a hallway that led to the chamber.

Once there, he turned on the overhead lights. There were no windows in this part of the building, so they were safe from everything but the noise.

Tam got to work instantly. She had a briefcase with her, which she wouldn't let anyone else touch. She zeroed in on some equipment he couldn't identify and the computer on the side wall.

All Eli and he could do was wait.

"What's that?" the reporter asked.

"Don't know."

"Does she?"

"Better than anyone on the planet, I'd wager."

"Wasn't she one of the scientists who came up with the weapon in the first place?"

Anger surged up inside Nate, but he just breathed for a moment, remembering Eli's position. "She was in the dark, just like we were. The only reason she's still alive is that she was smarter than all the rest. She figured out the big picture."

"She looks awfully young."

"That's because she is. Doesn't mean she's stupid." He looked pointedly at Eli. "You're younger than her by quite a few years."

"Point taken."

"I just wonder if you realize what you're in for."

"If you're trying to scare me, don't bother. Vince did a terrific job."

Nate smiled. He bet Vince did. "Why are you doing this? You could have just walked away. No one would have known the difference."

"I would have. Not that I think I'm some kind of hero. I just knew too much, I guess. Baker's notes were pretty complete."

"He helped us a lot."

"I hope I can, too."

"You wearing that bulletproof vest?"

"Shit, yeah."

"Good."

It was difficult not to watch Tam but keep his eyes on the door, to be ready for any of the different warnings that would alert him to get Tam and Eli out as quickly as possible.

She moved with such efficiency it was mesmerizing, but her safety was more important than his viewing pleasure.

Eli had calmed down, which just proved to Nate that he didn't truly understand the situation. If they were caught, there wasn't a chance in hell they'd live through the week. Omicron, with its roots in the legitimate CIA, could make them disappear just as they had all the scientists and doctors who'd originally created the chemical agent.

Nate wondered what they called it. VX07? Kosovo Juice? Instant Death?

Tam stepped back to the computer from the chamber and started typing. Engines revved, and before he knew it, a roar had taken over the lab. If security came within two hundred yards, the game was over.

If it was possible, he became even more alert. Nothing could go wrong now, not with the test, not with their plan. They couldn't be stopped. So much depended on it.

When Nate checked his watch, he was startled to see almost the full two hours had gone by. The chamber engines came to a gasping stop, and when Tam turned away from the computer he knew instantly that her antidote had failed the test.

"Let's get going," he said. "Time's almost up."

She nodded, her whole body showing her disappointment.

He brought his walkie-talkie up and clicked twice. It was his signal to Seth that they'd be exiting soon. If the coast was clear, Seth would click back.

Tam pulled some papers from the printer, then shut down the computer. Then she fetched some vials from the chamber, put everything neatly away in her case and said, "Let's go."

"What happened?" Eli asked.

"It didn't work." Tam passed him on her way back to the door.

"What didn't work about it?"

"We'll have plenty of time to talk once we're out of here," Nate said, herding the kid after Tam. He hadn't gotten the clicks, which worried him one hell of a lot.

Something had gone wrong. Security had heard the

engines, someone had been spotted. Whatever it was, he had to protect Tam and Eli.

They went through the offices once more, and Nate searched the grounds at each window they passed. He saw nothing. No new lights, no cars.

He held his people at the door as he opened it slowly. He heard a gunshot, and then a bullet slammed into the door frame inches from his head.

Nate jerked back, letting the door close, and flattened his body against the wall. He motioned Tam and Eli against the side wall so they'd be protected from whoever opened the door.

He couldn't hear the shots through the thick metal, but he definitely felt the impact as two more bullets slammed against the outside. He looked at the naked fear on the faces of his charges and grinned to let them know he'd get them out of this. He raised a finger to his lips in the universal symbol of silence, and they both nodded.

Desperately, he clicked the radio again, hoping against hope for a response. Maybe it had been a mistake to leave a one-armed man on watch.

He shook off the doubt. Seth's eyes were as good as ever, even if his confidence was down.

Nate clipped the radio to his belt and prepared for combat.

Where the hell was Seth?

16

HARPER HAD PICKED UP the phone three times now and hadn't dialed once. She was still trying to process what had happened this morning. Seth had been watching her. Protecting her. Even after all she'd said and done, he'd taken his whole day to sit in a truck and make sure she wasn't harmed.

At first she'd figured he was doing it for the good of the team, but that didn't make sense. The team had been told long ago that she manned the booth once a month, and no one had come. Which meant that Seth was there for her.

It was crazy. She wouldn't have returned the favor. He had to know that. She'd sent him off without a thought to his safety. All she'd cared about was her own little world.

What shook her was that she had no previous experience to help her deal with this. Even her parents had basically abandoned her when she was just a kid. She'd had to learn to take care of herself early and well. The only reason she'd become a doctor was that she'd figured she'd make good money at it—enough to take care of herself by herself.

Seth had no business watching out for her. She'd never asked him to. And she would have resented it if she didn't know that someone really was out to kill her.

It was only eight. There was still time to call. She picked up the phone again and this time she dialed.

"Hello?"

"Hi. It's Harper. I wonder if you have some time tonight to see me?"

EARLIER, AS SETH HAD watched Nate escort Tam and Eli through the jagged cut edges of the fence, he'd had some misgivings about being on this mission. But the self-doubt had receded with the excitement of being back in the game. As the clock ticked on, even that had dimmed from the sheer tedium of waiting. The third time he checked his watch and found that less than a minute had passed, he promised himself he wouldn't look again.

As he clumsily slipped on his night-vision goggles, cursing his prosthetic, Seth wondered how many places like this there were between Los Angeles and Long Beach. He was sure he and Nate had barely scratched the surface when they'd found chemical plants, paint factories, insecticide production facilities—not to mention that huge tract of fenced-off poisonous land in Inglewood. Jesus, if any one of these places had a serious accident, it would make Bhopal look like Disneyland, given the population of Los Angeles and the lax attitude most of the facilities had toward security. Sure, they all had 24-7 guard shacks at the entrance, but when had that ever stopped serious interlopers?

In short, he thought as he scanned the edges of the structures and buildings, this aging insecticide facility was not atypical. Tons and tons of biotoxins of various sorts, nearly as lethal to humans as to insects, and three people had gotten into one of their innermost labs in minutes.

The spot they'd chosen was nearly a mile from the guard shack, and from what he and Nate had determined, it took the security force nearly an hour to make their rounds. They'd been unable to determine what security they had in the labs, since most of the lights were on all night, making it difficult to tell if someone was patrolling the halls by following the flashlights.

The entire compound was surrounded by hurricane fence topped with razor wire, but security cameras were few and far between and, as near as Seth and Nate had been able to see, they had absolutely nothing really high-tech.

The fact that Seth had been able to pull Nate's truck—license plates obscured with mud—so close to a fence in the middle of the plant spoke volumes to Seth about their security.

Movement caught his attention, and he focused the glasses on the figure of a security guard coming around the corner of some kind of cracking tower—all huge pipes and peculiarly shaped levers and wheels. This time Seth did check his watch—and was startled to realize Nate and the others should be on their way out.

Without losing sight of the slowly approaching guard, Seth started the engine, then picked up the radio. He clicked the send button in the agreed-upon signal and waited for a response.

Nothing.

He tried again.

Still nothing. Shit, the one thing they'd been unable to check at all was if the radios would work inside the building.

He clicked the send button again. "Nate?" he whispered.

HARPER HURRIED TO THE door of the old Lincoln Heights house, trying hard not to actually scurry. Luckily Kate opened the door even before the first knock.

Once inside, she was surprised at how nice the place looked despite the building's age. She could tell that all the furniture had either come with the house or that they'd gotten it secondhand, because nothing really matched, but it didn't matter. There were pictures on the wall, mostly of Vince and Kate, but some of older people who must have been their parents. There was a really nice afghan on the couch, a big old TV and lots of books in built-in shelves. But it wasn't the furniture that made it so welcoming, it was the feel of the place. They cared about their surroundings, which was more than she could say about her house. "It's great."

"Mostly Vince's doing," Kate said, taking her coat and hanging it in the front closet. "He thinks we need to have things around us to remind us what we're fighting for."

"Interesting logic."

"I'm pretty sure he's right." Kate led her into the kitchen. "Coffee? Tea?"

"Tea, thank you."

Kate busied herself at the stove while Harper tried to figure out what the hell to say. This was entirely new for her. It felt as if she'd never confided in a friend before, but certainly she had. No one could reach the age of thirty-four without having one good friend.

"So you kicked Seth out, huh?" Kate turned and handed her a mug of tea.

"Well, that makes it easier to begin," Harper said, a too-familiar blush heating her cheeks. "Yeah, I kicked him out. Did he tell you about Smith?"

Kate nodded. She took her own mug and led Harper back to the living room, where they sat across from each other, Kate in a big green chair, Harper on the couch. "He saved your life."

"But he was also the reason Smith was a danger. Anything could have happened. There are innocent people working there who don't deserve to die because of what we're doing."

"But anything didn't happen. They may not be in uniform, but the guys are still Delta. They wouldn't have let anyone get hurt."

"You can't know that. It's not a situation of their choosing. There was no plan, no way of anticipating that Smith even had a knife."

"You're right. Someone might have gotten hurt. But I doubt very much it would have been a bystander. I've watched these guys in action and I've never seen them make a mistake."

"Except for the one."

"What one?"

Harper put her mug down on the coffee table without taking a sip. "The one that got us in this mess in the first place."

"You think they had a choice?" Kate asked, clearly shocked.

"I don't know. I wasn't there. I didn't see anything except the escape."

"The whole reason you're alive today is because of them. You think Omicron would have let you live, knowing what you do?"

"I didn't know the gas was government sanctioned until you told me. I found that village by accident. I didn't want any of this."

"Oh, and I did? Can you honestly tell me that knowing those villagers were killed by the U.S. is all right with you? That you would have turned your back rather than doing something about it?"

Harper sat back, the pressure in her chest so heavy she'd have thought it was a heart attack. But it was something else. An attack of conscience. "I don't know," she said, as honestly as she could. "I still have trouble processing that anyone could have killed so many innocent people, and for such a horrible reason."

"Well, then, what did you expect from Seth? He's been a soldier all his adult life. He's a real patriot, one who's willing to die for the principles. Losing his hand was like taking his gun away. It devastated him."

"It kept him alive."

"And we're all grateful for that. He didn't deserve to die."

Harper closed her eyes. Why had she come here? What did she expect from Kate? She hardly knew the woman.

"Why did you ask him to leave?"

She opened her eyes again even though she didn't want to. "I was scared."

"Of what?"

"That somehow Omicron would find the clinic. That people would be killed."

"Then why didn't you leave?"

"Me?"

"You've been a danger to your clinic since day one. Omicron is actively trying to find you. It's a miracle that we all haven't been killed. But you can't put this on Seth."

"But—"

"Harper, wake up. You're part of this whether you want to be or not."

Harper stared at the pictures on the mantel above the fireplace. She hadn't put up a single photo in her own home. Every wall was blank, just like her life. There was no one there, no one to care about. The fact that Seth cared enough to want to save her life was still difficult to compute. "I can't leave the clinic. They need me there."

"We need you here."

"I saved Seth's life. If you get hurt tomorrow, I'll do everything I can to help."

"I know you will."

"So where is he?"

"He's with Nate and Tam at some kind of laboratory where Tam's testing the antidote."

"Is it dangerous?"

"What isn't?"

"Point taken. When will they be back?"

"Don't know."

"And Vince?"

"He's there, too."

"You're not scared?"

"I'm scared all the time. But that doesn't stop me. I can't just curl up into a little ball and whimper."

"That's what you think I've done."

Kate shrugged. "I'm in no position to judge you, although I guess I have. Seth is a damn good man. It was hard to watch what you did to him."

Harper sighed, wishing…wishing she was someone else. "Once a month the clinic sponsors a booth at a street fair. We hand out condoms and educational material."

"I know."

"He came there today. To make sure I was safe. I said some pretty awful things to him."

"Oh," Kate said flatly, the single word filled with meaning.

"Yeah." Harper got her tea again and sipped the strong brew. It was good, just sweet enough.

"What are you going to do?"

She looked at Kate, her long, dark hair pulled back in a ponytail, her legs curled up underneath her. She seemed so sure. She'd grown up since Kosovo. "I'm sorry we didn't get to know each other better overseas."

Kate smiled. "I tried, you know."

"You did?"

"Remember all the times I asked if you wanted to get

something to eat? When I invited you to the late-night get-togethers at my apartment?"

She did. It hadn't been difficult to come up with excuses. She just didn't do that kind of thing.

"You chose not to get to know any of us. Even the men."

Harper hadn't been completely alone back then. She'd gone out with half a dozen guys, most of them medics or physicians. But nothing had come of it.

"I don't mean this to hurt your feelings," Kate said, "but I think you should hear this. Those guys weren't shining examples of chivalry. They talked. To the secretaries and the accountants, to the soldiers. And they weren't particularly kind."

"What did they say?"

"That you were safe. That you screwed like they would if they thought they could get away with it. Basically they figured they could get what they wanted from you with no strings, that they didn't even have to like you."

The words were like a gut punch, and she couldn't deny any of it. That's exactly how she'd been—how she was. All she'd wanted was sex, nothing more. No strings, no connection at all.

"I just think you might actually like Seth if you let yourself."

"I do like him."

"Really?" Kate shook her head. "Does he know that?"

"It's late." Harper stood, wanting out of there so badly it was all she could do not to run. "I'm sorry I've kept you up. And I appreciate the…tea."

"No problem. You know how to reach me."

They walked together to the closet and Harper donned her coat.

"He's staying with us now. Nate doesn't have the room now that Cade's here. Hell, he didn't have the room before that."

Nodding, Harper went to the door. She tried to think of something to say, but her thoughts were such a mad jumble. "Thanks."

"Don't be a stranger."

Harper let herself out, and when the door closed behind her, she felt desolate. As if she'd lost something big. Something she'd never realized she had.

NATE SLOWED HIS breathing and forced himself to remain calm. He could see Tam and Eli struggling to follow his example, but, knowing they didn't have his years of experience and training, he couldn't fault them for shifting nervously. He focused all his attention on trying to hear what was happening outside the door.

What he hoped was that the security guard would think the intruders had fled deeper into the lab. That way, his attention would be focused into the depths of the room rather than on the immediate threat—Nate right by the door.

The door handle turned and Nate tensed.

Slowly and with an amazing lack of sound, the door opened and a somewhat overweight, red-faced guard stepped in, peering toward the darkness at the back of the lab, his weapon thrust forward.

Nate stepped toward him, grabbed the man's right hand with his left and smashed him in the face twice with his right fist.

The look of surprise faded from his face as the guard slipped to the floor unconscious, his weapon in Nate's hand.

"C'mon," Nate said. He motioned to Tam and Eli. "We've got to get the hell out of here."

SETH'S HEART POUNDED. In other circumstances, he would simply have crept up to the guard and killed him. But the man was a civilian, and to do him any serious damage would make everything the government was saying about the team seem true.

Seth made sure the truck was in neutral, opened the door and slid out.

He ran lightly to the hole Nate had cut in the fence and slipped through. Staying close to the fence, he padded quietly toward a position near the end of the building.

He stood silently in the shadows.

He was so focused on the guard that they were both equally startled when the side door of the building burst open and Nate and the others came running out. Cursing under his breath, Seth leaped forward as the guard keyed his radio.

Although Seth and Nate had talked about it, they had not yet worked out any nonlethal moves for Seth with his new status. He ran straight at the guard and, with a great roundhouse right, clocked the man right in the jaw.

The man fell to the ground, dropping his radio, and Seth ran to join the others outside Nate's truck.

"I guess the radios don't work through these walls," Seth said.

"Might've worked out for the best," Nate said. "There was an inside guard, but he didn't call for backup." He turned to Tam and Eli. "Get in the back and stay down."

The two of them didn't hesitate, and when the door closed, Seth couldn't see them at all.

An alarm started in the near distance, and Seth took that as his cue to get the hell out of there. He headed for the passenger side, but Nate grabbed his arm. "Hey, you're the wheelman on this job," Nate said.

Seth looked surprised but pleased and quickly ran to the driver's side as Nate hopped in and closed the door.

The first of the security carts—not unlike golf carts—appeared from their right, and Seth grabbed the steering wheel with his prosthetic, shifted the truck into reverse and stepped on the gas, the tires spitting hard-packed dirt.

Heedless of the danger, the cart pushed through the cut fence and moved in front of the truck, a passenger with a bullhorn yelling, "Halt. Halt."

Seth shifted into drive and accelerated forward, swerving at the last minute so the bumper caught the cart and sent it spinning as the truck hurtled toward the front of the plant in the darkness.

It didn't stay dark for long, however. The entire front of the property was now well lit, and Seth saw a pair of the security carts racing toward him.

As they closed in, he switched on the headlights. And when the two carts parted, he shot directly between them.

Eli knocked on the sliding window that separated the cab from the truck bed. "You guys do this all the time?" he asked, voice quavering.

"Nah," Nate said. "We just do this for fun. Hell, when we get serious…"

"Listen," Tam said. The bantering stopped, and all ears strained above the sound of the powerful V8 engine.

"Sirens," Seth said. "They called the cops."

As the big pickup careened past the main gate, Seth hit the brakes, sending the truck into a controlled skid, which, not coincidentally, raised an immense and impenetrable cloud of dust. He stopped as the front tires touched the pavement of the Pacific Coast Highway, then turned quickly right, toward the sound of the sirens.

Driving carefully, at normal speed, he pulled into a gas station as the first police cars zoomed past, sirens wailing.

"I'll gas up," Seth said. "Nate, how about cleaning off those plates?"

"You got it," Nate said. He was grinning as he exited the cab.

17

THERE WAS ONLY ONE stop to make before Nate could head home. After Seth and Vince had gotten out at Lincoln Heights, he'd dropped Cade and Eli off at his place. Now he looked at Tam in the passenger seat. She stared straight ahead, her hands folded in her lap. She hadn't said a word since their escape, and he doubted she would. There hadn't been a chance to discuss the experiment. She'd said it had failed, but that was all. From her expression he knew it was bad. Not something she simply needed to tweak but a real blow to their plans. "Is there anything I can do?"

She shook her head. "It's over."

"What do you mean? The antidote doesn't work?"

"No, it works. But it has to be injected. Which is fine if you're the only one they're targeting, but that's not what they're doing. They're going to let this stuff out over whole villages, and unless we can think of a way to get an injector to every person, they're all going to die."

"Are you sure? Could you have gotten bad results? Maybe there just wasn't enough time."

"I'm sure, Nate. I'll admit I'm not an expert, but I

know how to read a gas chromatograph and a mass spectrometer. The antidote lost all effectiveness when exposed to oxygen."

"We'll think of something."

She turned to look at him. "We'll think of something? I've been in the horrible cave for the last eighteen months doing everything in my power to think of something. I don't have a solution. I'll never have a solution."

"Don't say that."

"Why not? It's the truth."

He got on the freeway and headed toward the lab. It was late, so the traffic wasn't bad, but he kept to the speed limit, as always. The last thing he needed was to be pulled over by a cop. What an ignominious end that would be. "What you need is rest. I can't believe how hard you've been working, and it's time to take a break. Maybe in a few days—"

"I still won't have an answer. Face facts, Nate. I'm never going to have a solution for this problem. I'm simply not equipped. The dispersal system is too far outside my expertise. I just don't know enough."

He reached a hand over and touched her arm. "You're goddamn brilliant."

"Smart doesn't mean I can know everything."

"You don't need to. We'll find someone to help."

"Bring someone else into this nightmare? No way. I wouldn't do that to my worst enemy."

"I know. It's been hell."

"Not just for me," she said. "For you, too. Especially you."

"We'll figure it out," he said, desperate to believe his own words. "If we can't get the antidote out there, then we'll have to stop things before it gets to that point."

"How?" she asked.

"No idea. But now that it looks like Boone located the manufacturing plant, we've got a better chance than ever."

She didn't respond. Probably because she couldn't think of anything positive to say. The plant was in Nevada and it was on restricted government land. It would be a bitch to get in there, let alone to take the place down. Besides, with what they were manufacturing, setting off an explosion would release the gas into the air, which would endanger countless lives.

They drove in silence, but instead of working the problem, his thoughts were on Tam. About how this failure was affecting her. She didn't deserve it. God, she'd worked so hard.

He got off the freeway and took a convoluted route to the lab. He didn't believe they were being followed, but he wasn't about to take any more chances tonight. They'd almost gotten caught. He doubted very much that any of them would last a night in jail. They'd be killed before their fingerprints were dry.

When they got to the condemned building, Nate parked, then got out with Tam. She walked slowly, and he could understand her reluctance to go down into that lab again. At least before, she'd had something to do, to keep her mind occupied. Now all she would see was how she'd fallen short of her goal.

"Listen," he said as they moved cautiously through the debris. "Start packing. Get all your material ready to be transported. I don't want you down there any longer than necessary."

"Where would I go?"

"I don't know yet. We'll figure it out. You just worry about your side."

She didn't say anything as they reached the door. He opened it and headed down first, his weapon drawn.

Her shoes were silent above him in the dark, but he could feel her there. Nothing felt off about the lab, and when he turned on the lights, it was just as they'd left it earlier.

Tam climbed down next to him and she looked around, too. He'd been right—she looked as if she were at a funeral.

"Want a drink?" he asked.

She shook her head. "Not tonight. I just want to crash. I'll talk to you tomorrow, okay?"

He hated leaving her like this, but he didn't want to push. "Okay. If you need me, I'm just a phone call away."

She tried to muster a smile, but it was badly done.

Nate touched her shoulder, gave it a gentle squeeze, then headed up in the dark. Tam didn't close the door until he had reached the top of the stairs.

He thought about her the whole way home, worry a tight fist in his gut.

SETH WOKE HER WITH A soft kiss on the forehead. Harper opened her eyes to find him sitting on the bed, and he was naked. Her eyes filled with tears as it sank in that he was back, that somehow in the two days since she'd kicked him out he'd seen that she needed his forgiveness. He smiled at her as he pulled the covers off her body.

She'd worn her old, ratty T-shirt to bed. And boxers. And she hated that she wasn't naked, too. She ripped the shirt over her head and felt his hands at her waist, teasing down the shorts.

The other thing she should have done was shave her legs, but Seth didn't seem to mind. With every inch of her skin he exposed, he bent over and kissed her there. Her belly button, her hip bone and finally the curls at the junction of her thighs.

Warmth spread through her. Warmth and hunger for more. Her shorts gone, she reached for Seth, and he lay down next to her, pulling her into his arms.

His kiss, when it finally came, was soft but sure. He knew where he was, who he was with. When he pulled away, she used the moonlight to look in his eyes. There was no anger. Only desire.

"Thank you," she whispered.

"For what?"

"For not listening to me. I was scared and stupid and I shouldn't have sent you away like that."

"Don't worry."

"How could I not? I was horrible."

He shook his head. "Never. I knew you were scared. Don't you think I know you by now? The way it's been for you? I know you try to push people away, but I'm not going anywhere. I'm here and I'm staying."

She clung to him, the feel of his skin like a balm, his scent an aphrodisiac.

His fingers moved between her legs, and soon she couldn't stop herself from writhing under his touch. How did he know her body like this? It was scary to be so open to another person. But then she remembered that he was her protector. He would keep her safe, not just in bed but always. Seth was her hero. Her champion. And she could let down her guard. Finally. After a lifetime.

He kissed her chin, the hollow of her neck, her breasts, each one. Not content with that, he trailed kisses down to her tummy and her mound.

His hands spread her legs and his lips replaced his finger. The perfect combination of hard and soft, his tongue was better than anything. He licked her over and over, and then the point of his tongue circled tightly over her clit until she gasped for breath and felt the beginning of her climax.

He shifted his body over hers, his knees between her legs, but the whole time he never let up with his talented tongue.

She gripped the pillows as she got close and closer, as all her muscles tightened, lifting her chest and pointing her toes.

When it hit, it was incredible. Tremors of pleasure, waves of release. He entered her in one swift thrust, making her cry out from the intense pleasure.

She prepared herself for his brutal rhythm, but that wasn't his plan. He moved slowly, languidly, in and out of her body, rubbing her sensitized clit in a way designed to make her insane.

Her fists loosened from their grip on the pillows and she let herself touch him. His hair, the dark stubble on his chin. She traced his lips with her index finger and watched as he swallowed. She stroked his shoulders and the top of his back. It wasn't enough, so she curled her legs over his lower back, feeling his movements in a whole new way.

"Tell me you forgive me," she whispered.

"There's nothing to forgive."

"Tell me that you love me."

"You know I do."

"Tell me you won't leave me."

"Never. No matter what. I'll always be here. I'll always keep you safe. No one will ever hurt you, not ever."

She wept as she lifted her hips, wanting all of him inside her, wanting this connection more than she'd ever wanted anything. They'd left her. They hadn't cared at all. But Seth did. He wouldn't go, he wouldn't hurt her, not the way they had.

His movements quickened and his arms tensed. Suddenly his head went back, and she could see the corded muscles of his neck as his rhythm got even faster yet more erratic. He was going to come and she wanted him to. She wanted him so much, so deeply.

He came then with a cry, straining as he emptied himself inside her. She clung to him, not ready for it to be over. It was the most peace she'd had in years. Maybe ever. "Please," she whispered.

"I'm here. Don't cry."

She hadn't even realized she was crying, but now the tears were hot on her temples. "I'm sorry," she said over and over, and he held her so tight.

He held her with both hands.

She woke in the bed, alone. The tears were real and her body felt as though she had come, but all the rest was nothing. A dream.

He'd never forgiven her. He'd never said he loved her. And she was more alone than she could bear.

The tears continued, and for a long time all she could do was try to catch her breath between sobs. But finally she was able to grab the tissues off the bedside and wipe her nose and her eyes. Her heart still raced, but she could swallow again and her eyes were open.

When she sat up, she realized it was the first time in months she hadn't dreamed about Kosovo. It wasn't a comfort.

She got out of bed, went to the bathroom. After she'd splashed cold water on her face, she padded to the kitchen and drank some water. Her gaze went to the clock. It was early. Five-thirty. Everyone smart was sleeping. She knew if she called, she'd wake Kate and Vince, and that wasn't fair. But she didn't think she could stand waiting even an hour. Hell, even a minute.

She got her cell from her purse and dialed Seth's number. Maybe she would wake only him. But her message went directly to his voice mail.

Okay, no way around it. She either had to wait for a sensible hour or wake Kate. She hoped Kate would understand.

She dialed. And waited. After six rings, a very sleepy Kate mumbled, "Hello?"

"I'm sorry. I know I woke you. But I need to speak to him."

"Who? Who is this?"

"It's Harper. I need to speak to Seth."

There was a long silence during which Harper imagined Kate getting out of bed to fetch Seth. But it was Kate's voice who finally answered. "Harper, Seth is gone."

"What?"

"He's gone to Nevada. To help Boone."

Her heart nearly stopped, but somehow she apologized, then hung up the phone.

She sat at her kitchen table, the only light in the room coming from the street. Seth had taken her at her word. She'd told him to get out, and that's exactly what he'd done.

It truly had been a dream. She had no reason to expect his forgiveness. She'd gotten exactly what she deserved. And she could hardly stand the pain.

THE DAWN LIGHT MADE Las Vegas look better than it deserved. The Stratosphere Tower, standing in the mountain's shadow, the glistening Mandalay Bay and all the spires and pyramids made for an unmistakable silhouette, one that would never be confused with a real city.

Of course, Seth knew that people lived in Vegas, he just didn't understand why. Not if they had a choice. And it was all about choices, wasn't it?

He checked the oil gauge on the old Ford Ranger. It

was a new purchase for Nate but a damned old truck. One that would probably break down before he reached his destination. That would be just his luck.

It seemed as though somewhere in the last couple of years he should have caught a break. He'd signed up for the Kosovo operation without suspecting a thing, he'd gotten his hand blown off and then he'd gone and fallen in love with a woman who could barely look at him.

Three days ago, he'd come to terms with it as he'd watched Harper in her ugly booth. Maybe they'd entice more kids to come by if the booth had some bright colors or some games or something. The way it looked now, it just reminded him of going to the principal's office. Which was beside the point. As he'd sat there in the bitter cold, his gun at the ready should anything come down, he'd faced facts.

Stupid as it was, he'd fallen in love with her. He'd tried to come up with a different explanation, but no matter how convoluted his thinking became, he always went back to the bottom line.

It was ironic, considering how deeply he'd hated her. He could still feel the fire burn inside him as he'd used every ounce of his energy to despise the woman who'd taken his hand. Yeah, he'd wanted her, too. But love? That was just plain dumb.

God knows she hadn't had any delusions. She'd said from the get-go that all she was interested in was sex.

But he was a sentimental ass and he'd let himself get attached.

It wasn't like the way it was between Boone and

Christie or Vince and Kate. They were at least normal. No. He had to fall for Harper. Who wanted no part of him, of the team, of their efforts to get their lives back.

She'd been happy. And then he'd come along and screwed it all up.

Of course, she was worried about the people at the clinic. She'd invested her time, her energy and her heart into that place. It made sense. She'd seen so much death that she wanted to fix people, heal them. She'd done exactly that.

What had he done?

He'd thought he was so clever. Disguises. They might have worked in some other situation, but not at the clinic and not when his picture was in every post office across the country.

He should have thought it through. He should have done his rehab alone, in private. It hadn't been worth the risk, not at six dollars an hour.

He'd left without cashing his check, which was just another bonehead move in a series of bonehead moves. Boone and Christie were as broke as anybody, and they all had to eat and buy gas and get the right equipment for the job.

Thoughts occupied by the task ahead, it was a good hour before he thought of Harper again. That was a record. He was on the other side of Vegas, on the 15 heading north. There was nothing but desert all around him. He passed the Moapa Truck Stop and Casino, then there was a whole bunch more nothing.

Harper was right there, right in the middle of his

head. It was worse because he kept thinking about how they'd made love and how she hadn't given a thought to the fact that he had only the one hand.

At least he knew she'd really wanted him. No way she'd faked that. To give her credit, she'd never lied to him in any way. She'd told him she wasn't interested in anything more than a screw.

It was time to start looking for his turnoff. He was glad it was coming up, because he hadn't slept all night. After the insecticide facility, he'd talked to Nate about his plans. The next day Nate had handed him the keys to the Ford and told him to keep in touch. No question about his ability. Everyone seemed to think he could do the job. Even Harper.

There it was, his turnoff. From the freeway it looked like a flyspeck of a town, but when he got onto the main drag he could see that the mountains had hidden a lot.

He remembered the directions to Boone's place, and it only took about ten minutes to get there. His new digs were at the Starlight Motel and Apartments. The place had seen better days. The pool in the courtyard was empty, the gate broken. There were three cars in the parking lot. He found number seven and parked by number twelve.

He got his duffel from the back of the truck and knocked on the right door. It was Christie, not Boone, who let him in, and she gave him a ferocious hug.

He remembered the first time he'd seen her, when Boone had gone to help her with the stalker. She'd been painfully thin and she'd looked like a prisoner of war. Now she was nothing but beautiful.

He hugged her back and felt a nudge on his leg. It was her dog, Milo. Damn, he looked good, too.

"Good to see you, Milo. How you been, boy?"

"Well, I can see where I stand in the pecking order."

Seth looked up to see Boone standing next to Christie. He had his arm across the back of her neck and a smile on his face.

Seth stood and shook his hand, then swore and pulled him into a hug.

"It's good to see you, man."

"You, too. It's been a long time."

Boone nodded. "We don't have much room here, but you can have the couch. You want coffee? Breakfast?"

"Sleep. I need a few hours, then we can catch up."

"Good enough." He took Christie's hand. "We'll be in the bedroom if you need anything."

"Thanks. Damn. I'm glad you guys are all right."

Boone slapped him on the shoulder before leading Christie away. Only Milo stayed to watch him wash and brush his teeth. He took off the claw and put it on the coffee table. Then he lay down without even taking off his shoes.

Harper was there when he closed his eyes. All he could think was that he'd finally forgiven her for saving his life. Now he couldn't forgive her for breaking his heart.

18

IN THE TWO WEEKS they'd been patrolling the manufacturing plant, Seth and Boone had made their way inside the perimeter, past guards, motion detectors, air patrols, heat detectors and boredom. Tonight's foray was all about the security cameras. They'd map as they went, of course, but their true goal was to get the make and design of the cameras outside the plant, diagram them, then find the power sources. It would be a long, tense night, but Seth didn't care. He needed the work, needed to get out of the motel room.

None of their progress would have been made had it not been for the bugs they'd installed months ago at Omicron headquarters in Los Angeles. There had been two major security meetings about the plant that had given them not only the locale, but the hierarchy of command. Nate had taped and transcribed them both, and the whole team had studied them until they knew everything but what an actual recon would reveal.

The most important fact was that this was a military operation, and if there was one thing Delta knew, it was how those things were run.

Boone was up ahead, crawling under a wire they'd cut last night. They had three minutes until they had to go flat, and in that three they should be able to get halfway to the main processing building.

The damn place was huge. Seth had a feeling they used to do a lot of munitions work here. There were safe rooms, exit strategies posted on practically every wall. Those were helpful as they provided some of the mapping.

The overall objective was to get as much information as possible so that a takeover could be successful.

How they were going to do that with their severely limited manpower was a question none of them could answer. The more intel they acquired, the better their chances.

Seth rolled under the wire, then made sure no one could tell that there was a breach. Then he belly-crawled toward the building, Boone just a darker shadow in the distance.

It was seven forty-five, and they were fortunate that night fell so quickly in the winter. And, at least for this part of the mission, he was fortunate to have the claw. It had proved very useful in the whole area of breaking and entering.

His watch alarm vibrated and he hit the dirt. The patrol would be by in a second, and he couldn't move a muscle until the sound of the Jeep's engine became a memory.

It was here, lying in a dry patch of desert, that it was the worst. Not the fear that they might be captured. Not even that they probably would be killed. It was Harper.

Two weeks, and he hadn't gone a day without her. Kate, who'd called him three times, had told him to get in touch with Harper, that it wasn't a lost cause, but Kate was in love and she thought everything had a happy ending.

Most of the time, he hoped Harper was miserable. He hoped she was tormented at the way she'd treated him, that she wanted nothing more than forgiveness and mercy.

Then he woke the hell up.

She'd said what she meant. Most people do, unless they're trying to get something they shouldn't have. She wanted him gone, and he'd granted her wish.

It hurt like a son of a bitch.

The good thing was they'd figured out the exact amount of time it took them to get back to the safety of the truck from wherever they'd patrolled during the night. That meant they worked until the last minute. By the time they were back at the motel both men were ready to crash hard.

Christie always made sure they had a decent meal, and Milo seemed thrilled each night that they'd made it home. They showered, stowed their gear, then Boone hit the bed and Seth hit the couch.

Christie had gotten herself a job as a waitress at a restaurant five blocks away from the motel, so she was gone while they slept. Luckily the motel only seemed to have the rare patron, so they weren't even bothered by noise.

Of course, he had his dreams. They were pretty much the same each day. Harper telling him to go. Harper with the knife at her neck. Harper in the bed, naked and smiling. That last was the toughest. He'd wake up sweating and hard, and it was uncomfortable to jerk off on Christie's couch, so he'd go to the bathroom. He felt like a twelve-year-old in there, but if he tried to ignore it, he would be awake until it was time to get up.

This was not the kind of operation that would cut any slack, so sleep was crucial. Eating well, keeping warm, good communication. It was like the old days. Only it sucked.

Finally it was safe to move again. He got up, stretched his neck and headed off at a dogtrot.

THE SUNRISE WAS THE only beautiful time in this part of the desert. Acres of scrub lay on either side of the highway, heavily trafficked by folks leaving Vegas, heading east. But Seth was too exhausted to give the sight much attention. They'd gotten a lot done tonight, but there was so much more to do. It felt impossible, but he wouldn't let himself go there. Getting out of Kosovo alive had been impossible. Fighting again after losing his hand had been unthinkable.

Falling in love had been the most unlikely thing of all.

TEN MINUTES FROM HOME base, Boone's cell rang. He'd turned it on the moment they were clear, as always, because from time to time Christie called. It was clear to Seth from Boone's immediate smile that it was her on the line.

"No kidding?"

Seth kept his eyes on the road and his thoughts on sleep, not his pang of jealousy at the contentment in Boone's voice. The two of them were happy, and he wouldn't have wished his old friend anything less. But, goddamn, it hurt. It was a knife to his gut, just like all the other knives that pierced as he watched the two of them touch or smile or kiss.

"No problem, honey," Boone said. "See you in ten."

Seth glanced over and saw Boone close the phone and put it in his vest pocket.

"She wants me to take her to the market before we hit the sack."

"So soon?" They'd done a shopping trip three days ago.

"Yeah. She forgot a couple of things."

That was the end of the conversation for the rest of the ride. It wasn't an uncomfortable silence, just a tired one.

When they pulled into the motel parking lot, Christie was standing outside room seven, purse in hand. She grinned at her lover, home from the wars, and met him as he stepped out of the truck. "Seth," she said, leaning around Boone, "I left something for you. And Milo's just come back in, so don't let him trick you into a walk."

Seth saluted. "Ma'am."

She climbed into the truck to take his place, and Seth headed inside. He couldn't decide if he was going to shower or eat first. Showering had more appeal.

He opened the door to the room, but he stopped just on the threshold. Because the something Christie had left for him wasn't dinner. It was Harper.

His heart slammed into fifth gear as he stared. She looked great. Jeans, sweater, her hair golden and wild. The way she looked at him made it hard to breathe.

"You might want to shut the door," she said. "The dog looks like he might bolt."

Seth saw Milo eyeing his escape, so he stepped the

rest of the way inside and closed the door behind him. "What brings you here?" he asked, hoping his voice hadn't really just quivered.

"I came to talk. If that's all right."

He nodded.

She headed to the couch and sat on the edge. He sat next to her, waiting, hoping like hell this wasn't just an encore to her last goodbye speech.

"I've been doing a lot of thinking," she said. "Mostly about what an idiot I've been."

He blinked, swallowed, found his throat dry as the desert.

"I want to apologize for what I said to you. I had no right to accuse you of bringing grief to the clinic. I did that all by myself. I should never have gone to work there. It was stupid. Suicidal. I knew Omicron wanted me dead, but I wouldn't accept it. I kept thinking it wasn't about me. I was so scared that all I wanted to do was hide. I thought I was invisible."

"I wish it wasn't so," he said.

"I know. You did your best to protect me, and all I did was give you grief. I've wished a hundred times I could take it all back."

"It's okay."

"No, it isn't. You saved my life."

"It was only fair. You'd saved mine."

"Best thing I ever did, and you'll never convince me it wasn't."

He looked down at his claw, dusty from his long night. He felt profoundly grateful that he hadn't died over it. For so long it had felt as if he'd never fight again, and now, after only this short time of practice, it had become a part of him. It would never be as easy as having his hand back, but he could be useful, and that's really all that mattered to him. "You were right to take my hand. Even if I had made it through, I wouldn't have been half as adept as I am with this."

"I'm glad."

He looked at her, wondering if she'd come all this way just to say she was sorry. Not that he minded—it was a good thing to hear. But it wasn't enough. Not for him.

"And there's something else," she said.

What's that?"

"I was really horrible when it came to…" She looked down at her shoes. "When it came to us."

"I don't know if I understand."

Her gaze came up to meet his. "I miss you, Seth. So much. We were just starting to get it right, and I blew it. I was hoping we could maybe try again."

"I have work here. I can't go back to L.A."

"That's why I quit."

"What?"

"Well, that's not the only reason. I quit the clinic because it was dangerous for me to be there. I quit because I kept looking for you in the break room. I wasn't any good anymore anyway. I kept thinking about you, about us, and I didn't want to be there."

"You left the clinic?"

She nodded. "I couldn't stay there, even if you don't want me around. It wasn't fair to them."

"You think I don't want you?"

She seemed a bit startled, but her gaze stayed steady. Then she touched him, four fingers on his arm. "Do you?"

He dislodged her hand, only to stand and pull her to him. She looked up, her lips slightly parted, her eyes wide and questioning.

Kissing her again was like coming home.

He'd thought about it so often, out there in the desert, how they'd not kissed enough. Not made love enough. He couldn't account for the way he'd missed her. But now he understood. It wasn't about how often. It was all about being with her.

Her small hands gripped him as if she'd fall from the earth if she let go. And that's the way she kissed him, too. As if her life depended on it.

He tried to give it back to her in kind, to let her know that she was welcome in his home, in his bed. In his heart. He wasn't good with words, but with his touch? At least, with his right hand.

It just felt so damn right to have her in his arms. Her body fit. The taste of her was better than anything he could imagine. This is how it was supposed to be.

She pulled back reluctantly, still holding on to him, but her eyes were more troubled. "There's more to say."

"After," he said.

"No. Now. Before I can't say it at all."

He didn't want to, but he let her go. They sat back down, Milo curled up right by his feet. It was dark in the room, with only one low-watt bulb in the lamp, but he could see Harper's face just fine. "Okay," he said. "Tell me what you need to."

She inched a bit away from him on the couch, and he could see how hard this was for her. His own chest tightened, not sure he wanted to know.

"The way it's been for me, always, is to get in and get out, fast, before I got in too deep. That part wasn't you, not at all. Just so you know."

"I couldn't help but notice you had your bags packed."

"Always. I never wanted to stick around because I never trusted another soul. Not since I was a kid." She ran a hand through her hair, making it messier—and sexier— than before. "Remember I told you about my father?"

"How he'd fleeced all those people?"

"Yeah. What I didn't mention was that it was my mother who turned him in. She was having an affair and she didn't want him around. So she called the FBI. After he went to jail, she broke off with the new guy and found another one. A lawyer who didn't want children. That's when I went to boarding school."

"You didn't see her much?"

"In the beginning, twice a year. That stopped when I was fifteen. I didn't see her again for two years."

"What happened?"

"She divorced my father, married the lawyer and had another kid. When she finally came to the school, she let me know she had a new family. The old one—me—was in her past. She'd gone on to bigger and better things."

"Shit."

"I'd always been independent, and from then on I

knew if I wanted anything out of life, I'd have to get it on my own. I got a full scholarship to college and a full boat on grad school. I worked during my residency, but I survived. But the trust thing was always there. Not just with men. With anyone."

"I can see that. It makes sense."

"Sense, yes, but you screwed it all up. I don't want to live the rest of my life alone. I don't want to mistrust everyone. I didn't even realize what I was missing until you were gone. It's no way to live, Seth."

"No. It's not."

"You know," she said, moving closer again, "I watched you call your folks one morning. You dialed the number, but you didn't say anything. I could see it hurt you terribly, but I didn't get it. I understood in a very logical way, as if I was watching a TV show or something. Now I see."

"No one should be alone like that," he said, hurting for her. "Not even someone so capable and strong."

"But I'm not strong. Not like you. I'm defensive and I react badly to other people's needs. That's why you can't just welcome me with open arms. I'm not good at this. Not good at—" she dipped her head again "—not good at loving someone."

"Loving someone? Are you sure?"

She nodded. "I used to make fun of people who said those words. Not out loud, of course, but inside I knew they were fooling themselves. That they'd pay for their romanticism. Now I see I was the one paying. I cut myself off from so much of life. It was like living in a half-world. And it was cold and empty."

He pulled her close on the couch, his arm around her shoulder, her head cradled in the curve of his neck. He ached for her and all he wanted was to make up for lost time. To shower her with everything she'd missed in her life. But that would have to wait. "I work every night," he said. "It's not like at your place. I don't have the safety of being wounded anymore. We have to win this. Or nothing matters."

"I'm here to help. In any way I can. Nate said in a while there's going to be a lot of electronics surveillance to do. I've been practicing. I'll never be as good as you, but if you'll let me, I'd like to be your hands. For the delicate work. All those surgery rotations weren't for nothing."

He kissed her again, letting himself sink into this new reality. Harper was here, was his. She wanted to work with him, be with him. A shadow thought came right then, and he pulled back, knowing he had to ask or it would worry him. "This isn't about your nightmares, is it?"

"No. I stopped having them the night you left. All I've been dreaming about since then has been you. God, Seth, I've wanted you so badly. I still don't know how I could have been so stupid."

"You have a strong sense of survival. It's a good thing. You're going to need it."

"So you forgive me?"

He looked deep into her blue eyes. "For what?"

She kissed him so hard they both fell back on the couch. As she lay over him, she kissed his nose, his cheeks, his eyes. Then she whispered, "I got us a room. Paid through next month."

"I think we'll have to get out of bed before then."

"Not if I can help it."

He smiled. "I've known for a while now, you know."

"What?"

"That I love you. That it was worth everything to be here right now."

Her eyes widened as she let that sink in. Before she could speak he kissed her again, knowing it was the utter truth. He wouldn't trade her for the world. Whatever it took, he'd make her safe. No matter what.

NATE RACED OVER THE broken boards and jagged rocks, past the crumbling walls of the old building, his heart nearly pounding out of his chest. He could hardly see for the sweat in his eyes, but he found the door. Open.

He climbed down, his gun in his hand, the safety off.

She'd called. It was Tam's number on his phone, so he knew it was her. All he'd heard was the gunshot.

He hit the floor running and he flipped on the light in the lab. He wanted to call out her name, but if they had her...

The place was a wreck. Tables overturned, file cabinets open, rifled. The whole place looked as if it had been hit by a tornado. She wasn't there.

He moved more slowly now, cautiously. Afraid that his fear would get her killed. As he moved toward her bedroom, he saw blood spattered on the floor, a beaker.

There, at the end of the hall, a body. He couldn't see if it was her. Just a shape in the dark.

And then he was blown halfway across the room as

the back of the lab exploded. He hit hard. His head cracked against the leg of a table. He was dazed for a few minutes, the heat building ferociously from the hall.

If he didn't get out now, he wouldn't ever get out. Forcing himself up, he had to wait for the dizziness to pass. Blood trickled underneath his collar, down his back. The fire would reach the exit in a minute.

He ran—lurched—to the stairs, then pulled himself up, feeling the heat through the soles of his boots. Then cold air hit his face, and he made it those last inches.

He stood, staring down into the fiery pit. Wondering if Tam was dead. Or, worse, if they had taken her.

* * * * *

Happily ever after is just the beginning…

Turn the page for a sneak preview of
DANCING ON SUNDAY AFTERNOONS
by
Linda Cardillo

Harlequin Everlasting—Every great love
has a story to tell. ™
A brand-new line from Harlequin Books
launching this February!

Prologue

Giulia D'Orazio
1983

I had two husbands—Paolo and Salvatore.

Salvatore and I were married for thirty-two years. I still live in the house he bought for us; I still sleep in our bed. All around me are the signs of our life together. My bedroom window looks out over the garden he planted. In the middle of the city, he coaxed tomatoes, peppers, zucchini—even grapes for his wine—out of the ground. On weekends, he used to drive up to his cousin's farm in Waterbury and bring back manure. In the winter, he wrapped the peach tree and the fig tree with rags and black rubber hoses against the cold, his massive, coarse hands gentling those trees as if they were his fragile-skinned babies. My neighbor, Dominic Grazza, does that for me now. My boys have no time for the garden.

In the front of the house, Salvatore planted roses. The roses I take care of myself. They are giant, cream-colored, fragrant. In the afternoons, I like to sit out on the porch with my coffee, protected from the eyes of the neighborhood by that curtain of flowers.

Salvatore died in this house thirty-five years ago. In the last months, he lay on the sofa in the parlor so he could be in the middle of everything. Except for the two oldest boys, all the children were still at home and we ate together every evening. Salvatore could see the dining room table from the sofa, and he could hear everything that was said. "I'm not dead, yet," he told me. "I want to know what's going on."

When my first grandchild, Cara, was born, we brought her to him, and he held her on his chest, stroking her tiny head. Sometimes they fell asleep together.

Over on the radiator cover in the corner of the parlor is the portrait Salvatore and I had taken on our twenty-fifth anniversary. This brooch I'm wearing today, with the diamonds—I'm wearing it in the photograph also—Salvatore gave it to me that day. Upstairs on my dresser is a jewelry box filled with necklaces and bracelets and earrings. All from Salvatore.

I am surrounded by the things Salvatore gave me, or did for me. But, God forgive me, as I lie alone now in my bed, it is Paolo I remember.

Paolo left me nothing. Nothing, that is, that my

family, especially my sisters, thought had any value. No house. No diamonds. Not even a photograph.

But after he was gone, and I could catch my breath from the pain, I knew that I still had something. In the middle of the night, I sat alone and held them in my hands, reading the words over and over until I heard his voice in my head. I had Paolo's letters.

* * * * *

Be sure to look for
DANCING ON SUNDAY AFTERNOONS
available January 30, 2007.
And look, too, for our other Everlasting title
available,
FALL FROM GRACE by Kristi Gold.

FALL FROM GRACE is a deeply emotional story
of what a long-term love really means.
As Jack and Anne Morgan discover,
marriage vows can be broken—but they can be
mended, too.
And the memories of their marriage have
an unexpected power
to bring back a love that never really left....

The real action happens behind the scenes!

Introducing

SECRET LIVES
OF DAYTIME DIVAS,

a new miniseries from author
SARAH MAYBERRY

TAKE ON ME

Dylan Anderson was the cause of Sadie Post's
biggest humiliation. Now that he's back, she's going
to get a little revenge. But no one ever told her that
revenge could be this sweet...and oh, so satisfying.

Available March 2007

**Don't miss the other books in the
SECRET LIVES OF DAYTIME DIVAS miniseries!**

Look for *All Over You* in April 2007
and *Hot for Him* in May 2007.

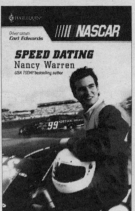

HARLEQUIN® *Romance®*

What a month!

In February watch for

Rancher and Protector
Part of the Western Weddings miniseries
BY JUDY CHRISTENBERRY

The Boss's Pregnancy Proposal
BY RAYE MORGAN

Also in February, expect
MORE of what you love
as the Harlequin Romance line
increases to six titles per month.

REQUEST YOUR FREE BOOKS!

2 FREE NOVELS PLUS 2 FREE GIFTS!

HARLEQUIN®

Blaze

Red-hot reads!

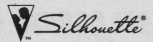

Silhouette®
Romantic
SUSPENSE

Excitement, danger and passion guaranteed!

Same great authors and riveting editorial you've come to know and love.

Look for our new name next month as Silhouette Intimate Moments® becomes Silhouette® Romantic Suspense.

HARLEQUIN®

Blaze™

COMING NEXT MONTH

#303 JINXED! Jacquie D'Alessandro, Jill Shalvis, Crystal Green
Valentine Anthology

Valentine's Day. If she's lucky, a girl can expect to receive dark chocolate, red roses and fantastic sex! If she's not…well, she can wind up with a Valentine's Day curse…and fantastic sex! Join three of Harlequin Blaze's bestselling authors as they show how three very unlucky women can end up getting *very* lucky.…

#304 HITTING THE MARK Jill Monroe

Danielle Ford has been a successful con artist most of her life. Giving up the habit has been hard, but she's kicked it. Until Eric Reynolds, security chief at a large Reno casino, antes up a challenge she can't back away from—one that touches her past and ups her odds on bedding sexy Eric.

#305 DON'T LOOK BACK Joanne Rock
Night Eyes, Bk. 1

Hitting the sheets with P.I. Sean Beringer might have been a mistake. While the sex is as hot as the man, NYPD detective Donata Casale is struggling to focus on their case. They need to wrap up this investigation fast. Then she'll be free to fully indulge in this fling.

#306 AT HER BECK AND CALL Dawn Atkins
Doing It…Better!, Bk. 2

Autumn Beskin can bring a man to his knees. The steamy glances from her new boss, Mike Fields, say she hasn't lost her touch. But while he may be interested in more than her job performance, he hasn't made a move. Guess she'll have to nudge this fling along.

#307 HOT MOVES Kristin Hardy
Sex & the Supper Club II, Bk. 2

Professional dancer Thea Mitchell knows all the right steps—new job, new city, new life. But then Brady McMillan joins her Latin tango dance class and suddenly she's got two left feet. When he makes his move, with naughty suggestions and even naughtier kisses, she doesn't know what to expect next!

#308 PRIVATE CONFESSIONS Lori Borrill

What does a woman do when she discovers that her secret online sex partner is actually her real-life boss—the man she's been lusting after for two years? She goes for it! Trisha Bain isn't sure how to approach Logan Moore with the knowledge that he's Pisces47, only that she wants to make the fantasy a reality. Fast…